THERE'S NO GRAVE LIKE HOME

A HORROR NOVEL

THERE'S NO GRAVE LIKE HOME

ERIN LOUIS

NEW YORK LOS ANGELES

Jacket design by Rejenne Pavon
Jacket Copyright © 2026 by Winding Road Stories
Interior Design by A Raven Design
ISBN#: 978-1-960724-58-8 (pbk)
ISBN#: 978-1-960724-59-5 (ebook)

Published by Winding Road Stories
www.windingroadstories.com

To all my OG's, my girls who know just what it's like to feel 60 at 25

1

Maggots. There was a time when she would have thought butterflies. But Georgia now thinks maggots. Crawling and squirming in an aggressive attempt to breach the sphincter in her esophagus. Her stomach flipped and she closed her eyes against the wave of nausea. They snapped open only a split second later to bring her back to the winding road. Her mind's narrative tried to look for the bright side, and she entertained the thought that she should be grateful for the sloshing of her guts as she drove past what she knew was the last fast food for miles. Years ago, she realized junk food was bad for business, but occasionally the craving still hit.

Once again, the voice in her head failed to comfort her with its pathetic attempt at positivity. She began to feel the need to stay impossibly skinny slipping away. The grip to hold the attention of men was loosening. She tried to take comfort in that thought also. She could stop and cram whatever monster burger and accompanying extra-large fries and drink they had to offer into her face. No, fuck the drink. She could pair the whole mess with an enormous chocolate shake. Her ass be dammed. Her stomach too. It wasn't just the fear of stretchy pants and cellulite. After all, once you pass forty, cellulite is just a given. There's no amount of tofu and quinoa that will stop its inevitable advance. But years of occasional binging and purging has left her stomach inhospitable to anything a fast-food restaurant had to offer. There wasn't a cheeseburger in the world that wouldn't set her stomach on fire and cause her pants to constrain her in the most unflattering of ways.

The road to her father's house twisted under a canopy of trees. The leaves painted her windshield in a tie died pattern of shades of greys and bright bits of sunlight. She put herself in the moment and pressed on the gas to spite her dread of actually arriving. She worked her ass off for this car, and it was made for roads like this. The last time she had driven it, she was coming in the other direction in a busted-ass Pontiac with no air conditioning and a cigarette burn hidden under the purple fuzzy seat covers. The only thing her first car had in common with the one she drives now was the heavy metal that vibrated the speakers.

Geogia pressed the button which opened the sunroof on the black BMW her father would have hated. That's not why she bought it, but somewhere deep down she knew otherwise. The cool air sucked her blonde hair out the top of the roof and she sped up. The turns came fast, and although it had been almost two decades since she was last on this road, she remembered all of them. Challenging herself to take them even faster, she pressed harder on the peddle. The maggots squirmed again.

It had only been a few weeks since she had gotten the call that her father had passed. Died. She hated the word passed. Passed into what? The ground? He was dead, and that was it. There was no funeral. No point in it. Not like he'd have known if there was one or not. Funerals benefit the living not the dead. Georgia didn't think he was looking down on her from a paradise in the clouds. Or looking up at her from where hellfire burned eternal for that matter. Just dead. He always told her that she would be a believer again someday. That she would find her way back to God's light. That she would be sorry if she didn't. She wasn't dead yet, just middle aged. Although, in stripper years, forty-five was as good as dead. In human years, with a little luck, she figured she was just about halfway to dead. And she was still a long way from sorry. Georgia couldn't imagine believing in, let alone worshipping any god, especially one that demanded love in exchange for the privilege of not burning eternally. She wasn't going to be emotionally exploited by any guy, deity or not.

Georgia was twenty-five the last time she had seen her father, and thirty the last time she heard his voice. She received cards every Christmas up until ten years ago, when she assumed he had finally given up. Each one was stamped with a cross or bible verse, sometimes with the crucified dead guy on it, and sometimes not. Each one went unopened into the recycle bin. She hoped they'd be turned into cheap toilet paper, like the empty promise of comfort and cleansing they were.

Her parents split soon after she was born. Georgia's mother raised her alone with her sister, Grace. Her father sent them gifts and occasionally showed up for the holidays, dragging the three of them to church—an act they all resented, but one that her mother insisted on. She said that it was his way of having a relationship with them, his way of being a father. Her mother wasn't religious. A hopeful agnostic, maybe. But she had once told Georgia, that she didn't know how else to connect them with their father. It was the only interaction she hadn't had to beg him for. He was absent every other time despite being close in proximity. As there had been a time when she thought of butterflies in her stomach, there had also been a time when she thought that she would have a relationship with her father. As a kid, well into her teens, she sent him homemade cards and called him on the phone, only to be greeted with awkward silence if not nothing at all. The last time she had come up to this town to visit, she finally found the balls to tell him how she felt. Describing her vision of trips to the zoo, or to the ice cream shop. Making smores in the woods, her smiling father teasing her for not wanting to touch the slimy fish she had finally caught. Long talks about life and the future. Visions of the father she saw on sitcoms and commercials but hadn't yet got to know. The father she had convinced herself lived somewhere in this man who had donated his DNA to give her life. As she began to cry, he handed her a handkerchief from his pocket and walked away.

The wind sucked more of her hair out into the cool mountain air. Her old Pontiac hadn't had a sunroof, but the last time she was on this road the windows were rolled down. The scent on the wind hadn't changed; old memories filled her head as the air filled her lungs. She let off the gas. Acutely aware of how close she now was to her father's house. Her house. Having only been there a few times, despite living in the same town.

As the road narrowed, speed was no longer an option. The curves didn't scare her, the chance of another car coming in the opposite direction did. It had taken only one close call as a new driver to learn that lesson. The jolt of the gravel under the thin-skinned tires of her dilapidated car as she swerved to avoid being clobbered by an old pickup, was enough to take the fun out of the drive. Not enough to take all of the joy out of taking these mountain curves at breathtaking speeds, but the roads, if they could still be called that, narrowed as they drew deeper into the residential portion of the county. A truck lurking on the other side of a bend could appear at any moment. She slowed to what felt like a crawl, barely enough to startle the deer snacking on the weeds at the side of the road. The doe looked up at her as she passed. Georgia shuddered.

Less than a mile away, her speedometer indicated she had around three minutes before the fence that lined her father's property would come into view. Her property. The lawyer who had handled her father's estate would be there waiting. It was her final and pretty much only task left. Georgia recognized the woman's name but couldn't bring up her face. The town of Blackberry Ridge boasted a feed store, a café, an elementary school, a church, and exactly one stop sign. The latter was only added after months of contentious town meetings and a particularly nasty accident at the intersection. Progress was not easily welcomed in Blackberry Ridge. Her father had been screaming about it the very last time they spoke. He was still yelling when she hung up on him. That was the last time they had spoken, nearly fifteen years ago.

The fence to her father's property hid behind a fresh coat of white paint. The wood's new makeup didn't fool Georgia. She turned into the driveway and the maggots danced in her stomach. A redheaded lady stood next to a late model Lexus parked next to the garage. The face that went with the name she had recognized came into focus. Shelley Mather. She was in the class above her, and they had barely spoken. Not a friend, and not an enemy. Shelley hadn't been anything but another face in school.

Georgia sucked in a breath as she pulled up next to the Lexus and parked. Shelley wore a lawyer's smile that matched her beige pantsuit and loafers. Heels would be silly up in this part of the country, a fact that Shelley made clear as her eyes darted briefly to Georgia's kitten heeled black mules as she opened the door to her car.

"Hello! How was the drive?" Shelly said in her lawyer's voice which contradicted the image of Shelley's likely long dead Rainbow Bright lunch pail. Georgia blinked to wash away the memory.

"Good," she replied. She attempted a smile, but it morphed into a lie, "relaxing," Georgia's shoulders were in knots.

"Great time of year. So sorry to hear about your father,"

Shelley lied back. No one in this town was sorry he was dead. Maggot food.

"Thanks." Georgia gave up on the smile as her eyes turned to the house. They crawled over the garage to the front door, and to the large realtor's lock that hung on the knob. The maggots multiplied and grew even more restless as Shelley spoke.

"I have all the paperwork and keys here. Just need your signature, and that will be it. Again, sorry for your loss." The last part came out coated in a kind of patronizing goo. "Your mother and your sister too."

"Thanks." The maggots turned to stone.

"Uh…If you could just sign here." Shelley opened the manila folder that sat on the hood of her car and dug into the handbag that hung from her shoulder. She produced pen that bore her name and phone number on it and handed it to Georgia. She took it and signed where Shelley held a short, but well-kept fingernail. "In the back of the file, you'll find the numbers for the utilities. As you know, this property is on well water, so you won't need that. The electricity is still off, but the generator is full and should suffice until you make arrangements to have it turned on again. And of course, no cable, but the satellite TV isn't all that bad." She paused. "Here are the keys. I'm happy to come in with you, if you would like." Another lie. Her face said she wouldn't be happy at all to enter the dead weirdo's home.

"No that's ok. I'm not planning on staying long. Are we all good here? Is there anything else?" Geogia peeled her eyes away from the front door.

"That's it. The whole thing was pretty simple as we discussed on the phone." She shifted uncomfortably in her sensible shoes and began to open the door to her sensible car. "Are you sure you don't want me to come in with you?" She said, as she put the key in the ignition and turned it. The girl with the Rainbow Bright lunchbox had found her calling as a professional liar. Not that Georgia had any stones to throw in that department.

"No. I'm fine. Thank you for all your help. I really appreciate it," Georgia made the only truthful statement in this awkward conversation.

"You're welcome. Great to see you!" Shelley lied once more, although this time she had to yell it, as her tires kicked up gravel.

Georgia didn't wave or watch her drive off. Her eyes had gone back to the door of the house. It looked as freshly painted as the fence. The blue paint on the eves held a shine that indicated it probably hadn't seen winter a winter yet. The siding looked to be new as well. She walked up the path and toward the large lock on the door, stepping deliberately on the large crack in the concrete. A crack she had dutifully avoided as a kid, and her mother's back had broken anyway. She shook her head to clear the thought.

She told herself to get a fucking grip, as the key weighed heavy in her hand. Time to let go of the dramatics. This could end up being a really good thing for her. The house was worth enough for her to transition to more traditional employment as she pleased. The timing couldn't be better for her. Thanks dad. The maggots came to life and squirmed again in her stomach.

"Get fucked," she said to them as she turned the key and popped the lock.

2

THE SMELL of rotting flesh clogs her nostrils as the door creaks open. Spiders, not scrambling away in terror at the invasion of the daylight, but drawing close, malice reflected across a thousand tiny eyeballs. Georgia's stomach fell into her crotch and a million maggots fell with it.

She shook her head and opened her eyes to the still closed door in front of her. The cool hard doorknob still unturned in her hand. She rolled her eyes back as if she could give a dirty look to her own stupid, paranoid brain. She turned the knob, and the door slid open without so much as a whisper.

The front door sat under an eve, which in turn sat under a large oak tree. Shaded from the sun and heat, it was cool and almost dark as she stood at the threshold. The foyer stood warm and bright in contrast, bathed in sunshine. No rotting bodies or spiders. The right flank of the house was a wall of windows which allowed the sun to decimate the dark vision her brain insisted on conjuring up. She laughed, remembering the green tendrils of the aggressive house plants her father had kept here. This was her favorite room in her father's house. She thought it still was, even without the greenery. The entire room was bare, as was the rest of the house.

The call she received from Shelley a few weeks ago had been short and sweet. It wasn't the news of her father's death that had shocked her, but her own lack of emotions. If she was surprised at all, it was that she had been named in his estate at all. Or that he even had an estate to leave. But he had thought ahead, and maybe most surprising of all, he had thought of her. It would have been easy enough to simply leave everything to his church. Instead, he left this house, free and clear to her. Everything pre-arranged. Shelley had recommended a cleaning service that would come in and sort, pack, and dispose of everything in the house. What could be sold would be sold. What couldn't be sold was either donated or thrown away. But when they got there, they discovered the place was completely empty. Dusty, but empty. No dishes, or furniture, no personal effects at all.

She stepped inside and inhaled the caustic but welcome scent of bleach. Scrubbed clean, Georgia almost couldn't believe she had ever been here at all. Her memories of the place now seemed like dreams. She turned to the left and walked into the kitchen. Fresh tile, she didn't recognize lined the floor. She couldn't imagine even one meal had been cooked on the glittering stovetop, or a dirty dish ever having disgraced the sink. The scene overlapped the vision of her dated apartment kitchen, done entirely in split pea green, and cream-colored ceramic.

The kitchen didn't so much end, as seep into a small dining area that bled into an equally small living room. The wall that divided the spaces had disappeared like a phantom. As had the carpet. New vinyl flooring doing a magnificent job pretending to be hardwood absorbed the fall of her heels. Sunshine bounced jovially off the freshly painted walls in blatant irreverence of the dead former occupant.

Georgia struggled to pull memories of her father into the space and failed. Four decades he had lived here, and she had only been in his home a few times. A slight glimmer of guilt laced its way through the now dying maggots in her guts. She wasn't afraid anymore, she wasn't apprehensive, or filled with dread now that she was here, and the paperwork signed. There was nothing. No grief, no melancholy. But her brain kept insisting that there should be, and that she was an asshole for the voice in her head chattering away about home values and what she might do with the proceeds.

She gave up on trying to restore the memories of her father. They died well before he did. She instead focused on the newness of everything in the house. The cleaners had obviously done a bang-up job, but they hadn't remodeled the whole place. Her father must have. And very shortly before he died. Which begged several questions, none of which had any clear answers. The only bank account he had was a checking account, which she had closed without bothering to look at any of the statements. There hadn't been more than a few hundred dollars. She didn't think there was any point to it. But now as she looked at the gleaming new fixtures, and fresh paint, she began to wonder where the money had come from. Cash, she suspected. Likely unreported. Georgia had no stones to throw in that department either. Probably not much of a mystery. And given his profession, he likely did most of the work himself.

Her father worked as a handyman, self-employed, but that was all she knew. She had asked him about it, a feeble effort to form some sort of bond with him but was stonewalled. *Hey dad, so nice to be self-employed, amirite?* Eventually she just stopped caring. She learned more about his life after his death than she had her entire time on earth. And much of that, no, all of that was nothing more than rumors and supposition. Her mother never refused to tell her more about her father, but she didn't shed much light on him either. At some point, she just assumed there wasn't that much to know. Georgia intended to push the issue but thought she had plenty of time and put it off. And then time simply ran out.

Georgia moved on to the hallway which led to the bedrooms. The first bathroom gleamed with its own pride and ignorance of human waste. Her stomach swam. Not with apprehension and dread, but curiosity. She wondered if the cleaners weren't as good as she first thought, but that they didn't have much work to do. Farther down the hall, she moved to the first bedroom, which held no surprises. It appeared to be as unlived in as the rest of the house. Any and all evidence of his existence had been wiped clean.

The master bathroom was much like the first, empty and barren. Giddy butterflies replaced the maggots in her stomach. She might just make a killing on this sale. The wrinkled smiling face of Pete appeared in her mind. Her favorite mark from the Tuesday night shift at the club would likely pay well over her asking price for the fucking place. She wouldn't even need a realtor. With any luck, the old dude would pay cash. Still lost in his delusion that she would someday finally sleep with him.

She couldn't stifle the giggles as she walked around the empty but immaculate room. Suddenly she was excited about her father's untimely passing. *Father* was as stupid of a word as *passing* was. He was dead not *passed*. And he hadn't been a *father*. She saw him lying on the floor in the middle of the room. She couldn't know if the vision in her head was accurate. Shelley told her that he had been found in this bedroom by a neighbor. No foul play suspected at his age. Just an old dude who blew a fuse or sprung a leak from something important. The body faded away.

"There is no father, only Ronald. And now there isn't even that." she said to the empty room, as she walked back into the hallway. Any lingering guilt she felt about her lack of feelings for the dead guy had died with him. She didn't know the guy, and never would.

Lost in her thoughts, Georgia screamed when she felt the ghost, phantom, demon spirit from hell, touch her bare calf. A thousand nightmares rushed through her brain, some remembered and some simply conjured by her imagination. She stumbled and ran face first into the wall in the hallway. A loud screech pierced her ears, and she squeezed her eyes shut, expecting impact. She opened them to a wide-eyed, scruffy and scrawny grey cat staring back at her.

Her heart lurched, and she slouched against the wall. The cat rubbed on her legs, and meowed. She slid all the way down until her ass was on the floor and extended her legs. The cat saw its opportunity to perch on her lap. It stretched its neck to rub under her chin. Its purrs nearly shook the fresh vinyl flooring.

"Where in the actual fuck did you come from?" The cat looked at her as if it didn't know either. She scratched its head. Her hand moved to the moldering collar on its neck, from which dangled a name tag which read 'Ralph' and nothing else.

She plucked Ralph off of her lap, attempting to brush the grey cat hair off her black capris, only succeeding in shuffling it around. She stood up, intending to close the window from where Ralph must have gotten in. She went back through the house checking each window and door and found them securely closed. Ralph followed her, still purring. She looked down at him. She could see the knobs of his spine through his short fur. She hadn't seen any signs of life in the house. Neither human nor feline. No food or water dishes, and with the whole place closed up, she certainly would have smelled a cat box. Ralph only stared at her and offered an undecipherable meow. She frowned at him in return.

Georgia pulled her phone from her back pocket and thought about calling Shelley, but slid it back in place without opening the lock screen. Their brief encounter hadn't given her the impression that she was in a hurry to help any further. Georgia knew of the rumors about her dad. The town weirdo and recluse. She didn't know much about him, but she did know plenty about the town. Gossiping middle school kids turned into bored adults, either too dumb or poor to leave the town they grew up in. The truth was always more boring than the fantasies conjured up in a town without cable TV.

The closest neighbor was more than a half a mile away. Not too far for a cat, she was sure, but Ralph looked almost emaciated. She didn't think he'd seen a meal or a vet in some time. He looked up at her, and while cats had never quite been her thing, a warmth bloomed behind her aging silicone implants.

"Well, fuck me sideways Ralph."

Ralph followed her to the front door but refused to follow her out of it. She picked him up, but he began to hiss at her as she tried to take him outside. Stopping just short of shredding her with his untrimmed claws. He calmed down when she stepped back inside.

"Bro, I can't leave you in here," Ralph began to purr. She put her foot outside the door and his purr turned into a threat. "Fuck."

Stepping back inside, Ralph nuzzled under her chin. If he could talk, he would have told her that she could in fact, leave him here. She looked down at him, unsure what to do but knowing that trying to sell a house, no matter how pristine, that smelled of cat piss would throw a wrench into her plans.

"Alright dude, you gotta go," she said and thought she saw the glimmer of a frown on Ralph's face. She stepped back inside and stood behind him. Ralph turned to face her, staring up at her with his yellow eyes. She stepped toward him, shooing him with her hands but not touching him. Ralph only stared. He didn't budge.

It had been years since she had been into town, but she didn't wonder if the feed store was still there. She knew it was. Just as she knew the guy who had felt her up one drunken night in eighth grade would be behind the counter or stocking shelves. Mike. His hands were rough and soft at the same time. He had squeezed her nipples in a way that dampened her panties and brought a blush to her cheeks. In the dark, she had thought he was someone else. But David, her real crush, was making out with another girl instead. She felt stupid and ashamed when her mistake became apparent. But the memory of Mike's hands had kept her company when she was alone for years after.

Ralph plopped down in the foyer, deciding he would lay his ground rather than stand it.

"Fine, I'll be back. Try not to shit on anything."

She glared at him as she stepped over the top of him and closed the door. She didn't bother to lock it. It wasn't like there was anything in there to steal. Not to mention it was out in the middle of nowhere, and out here, people weren't likely to walk down a driveway and definitely not into a house where they hadn't been explicitly invited. The likelihood of catching a load of buckshot to the chest was far too high to risk stealing anything. She sighed as she started her car and headed into town.

3

GEORGIA ROLLED down her windows and allowed the crunchy guitar and booming drums to assault the quiet air of the main street. She hated almost everything about this place, and the fact that they couldn't come up with something more interesting to call the main drag than Main Street only served to piss her off more. It was unusually wide. Lined with small shops, and ancient buildings. The town had burned twice since being established. Both times, the fire jumped from one side of the street to the other. Georgia thought the damned place should have taken the hint, fucked off and given the land back to the deer and mountain lions. But instead, they simply widened the street so that the next fire would only be able to burn one row of buildings instead of the whole town. To Georgia's dismay, that theory had not yet been tested. But a girl could hope.

The early afternoon sun cast short shadows on the pickup trucks and SUV's that lined the road. The door to the fire house stood open, as two men in overalls sprayed the town's only fire truck with a tiny garden hose. A nauseatingly sweet scene straight out of a Norman Rockwell painting. As a freshman in high school, she had walked in there on the advice of the school counselor to ask about becoming a paramedic. Wide eyed and excited at the idea of being a first responder. Albeit an idea that she knew now would have likely faltered with time. Every door had been open to her then, she wanted to explore, to test out every option.

"You want to be what?" The last word struggled to get out of his mouth, before the fire chief vomited contagious laughter that boomed through the station. Fresh humiliation sprouted as the memory she had thought she had buried with the long dead man resurfaced.

"Fucking asshole," she said under her breath. "God, I fucking hate this town."

The feed store was exactly where she had happily left it more than a decade before. She almost drove passed it and out of town, but Ralph's face made her park instead. She was only going to go in, find a box or carrier, and an address to take him to. She would pretend to not know Mike, if he happened to recognize her. Once the damned cat was delt with she could get started on dumping the house and moving on from this place for good.

A cowbell clanged as she pushed open the door to the feed store. The young man behind the counter was not Mike. Georgia let out the breath she didn't know she was holding. She breathed in the sawdust from the floor along with the lingering scent of manure that lived behind the wooden building in a large shed. Some kids in her class claimed to love that fresh earthy smell. To Georgia it just smelled like shit.

She looked around the room, Not-Mike was doing a magnificently terrible job of not staring at her. She kicked herself for not just going around to the dumpster next to the shit shed and plucking a cardboard box out of the trash. She could just Google a shelter and drop off the cat, or maybe even just at a vet. But here she was, and she would not allow herself to look like a coward. What the hell was she so afraid of, anyway?

Pimple faced Not-Mike, pointed and laughed at her. Georgia closed her eyes against the laughter that was only coming from inside her head.

Georgia pulled her shoulders back, letting her fake boobs lead the way to the counter. Her city shoes sinking slightly into sawdust and what was probably cow shit that lined the floor as she stepped toward the counter.

"Hello," she started strong, but her words caught in her throat. She cleared them with a clandestine growl, "I just bought the house up the hill, and there is a stray cat there. I need to get him out of there."

"Ron's house?" Not-Mike said, he lowered his eyelids indicating he wasn't really asking a question.

"Uh yeah, do.."

He cut her off.

"Your dad. Real weird…." Not-Mike didn't finish.

"That's enough Michael," a voice came from the back room behind the counter. "Georgia! How good to see you!" Mike said.

Georgia's nipples poked the inside of her bra, thankful for the padding, but dismayed at the fact that she had nothing hide her blush. She flipped the switch that put her in performer mode. A translucent facade she had perfected through years of dealing with drunk bachelor parties. A mask that was mostly her, but not all the way. Her not-quite-Georgia mask.

"Oh, hey Mike! Wow, so good to see you." *Meryl Streep, eat your heart out*, she thought.

"So sorry about your father……and you know."

Her words tried to catch in her throat again, but she swallowed them. Mike's eighth grade face bled through the roadmap of lines and sun damage of the last couple of decades. She couldn't help but see the round freckled face of the boy who had felt her up.

"It's ok. But apparently, he had a cat."

"Ralph. I made his tag a couple of years ago," Mike smiled.

Mirroring his smile, she said, "Yeah, Ralph. Scared the piss out of me." She produced a surprisingly real sounding fake laugh. "I was hoping you might know a place I can take him?"

Mike put a dirty fingernail to his lips, and his eyes turned upwards, "The shelter over on Ginger Blossom Rd is closed most of the week. It opens again on Friday."

Georgia didn't have two days; she wanted the thing gone. She knew of a shelter near her, but with the shape Ralph was in, he'd be first in line for the forever nap of the strays. She wanted him gone, but not that gone.

"Shit…" She cringed, "Well, do you have a carrier I can use? And I guess some supplies to last him until Friday?"

"No." He said deadpan. Georgia frowned, and opened her mouth, but was interrupted by Mike's laugh. His eyes laughed along with his mouth and only served to bring forth his kid face again which refused to stay hidden behind wrinkles and time. "Of course I do, silly."

She smiled, then mimicked his laugh, "Oh? Glad I got the right place."

All she wanted was to get the hell out of here, set the cat up for the next couple of days, and get back to her shit box of an apartment mercifully surrounded by concrete and light pollution.

"Hang on, I'll be right back," he said before disappearing down one of the isles.

The kid, formally known as Not-Mike, but now Micheal, no longer staring at her face. Now he was just staring at her tits. She sneered at him, but he didn't flinch. Georgia turned her attention back to the isle his father had gone down, wishing she could simply will him to hurry the fuck up.

"So….I heard you were a….." Formerly Not-Mike began.

"Micheal!" Mike yelled as he emerged from the isle with an

arm full of cat supplies, "Someone knocked over the collar display again."

The boy shut mouth and gave her tits one long last look, before walking away.

"Alright, this should do. How long are you planning on staying?"

"I'm not," she said, slipping out of performer mode. She flipped the switch again. "I mean, I have a lot going on at home," she lied. She had exactly nothing going on at home. She wasn't even sure she had a job anymore. Technically she had a job, but weekend night shifts were now fraught with twenty-somethings asking her how old she was. She had been thirty-five for around a decade already and even the drunk dudes were starting to doubt her. The dark lighting and fake smoke could only hide so much. Father Time is an unforgiving son of a bitch.

"That's too bad. I was hoping we could catch up," his eyes darted to her boobs. Like father like son. He placed the cat supplies in a cardboard box without ringing her up, then slid one of the business cards into the box. "On the house. Let me know if you change your mind." He said with a smile that if she didn't know better, could have passed for genuine.

"Thanks," she said, managing to keep her mask up. "Nice seeing you," and she almost meant it.

She picked up the box with a smile and nod, before walking out. Georgia felt his eyes burning a hole in her pants as the cow bell sang her exit.

Ralph was lying in the exact same spot as when she left.

"Hey Ralph, you stubborn little fucker. Got some stuff for you."

She went to the farthest corner of the foyer and set down the box. She took out a litter box, cat litter, a water and food dish, a small bag of cat food along with a small cat bed. Ralph sniffed the bed, then hopped into the box.

The sun was going down as she finally got the cat settled and drove up the driveway and out of the town she had hoped to never see again. She'd be back in two days to take the cat to the shelter. In the meantime, she would make the arrangements to sell the house and figure it all out from there.

There were no maggots as she sped through the hills toward her little apartment. The fast-food joint she had passed on the way there was still open. *Fuck it,* she thought as she pulled in the drive through.

4

THE WHITE "THREE day pay or quit" notice taped to her apartment door glowed under the small porch light.

"What the fuck, Pete?" She said too loudly as she ripped it down and crumpled it in her fist.

She tossed her car keys on the counter in the kitchen and pulled her phone from her back pocket. She typed in the words she had spoken aloud. Already knowing what his response would be before he answered didn't help when it actually came.

I'm sorry hun. I just couldn't do it this month. Ran into some tax stuff and my dad needed help too. Not sure when I will be able to help again.

Georgia resisted the urge to throw her phone, a small effort compared to the will it took not to tell Pete to eat shit and die. But although she knew he was pretty much writing her off for good, she didn't think it was a good idea to burn this bridge. She knew it was coming. It was over a year ago that he started to share his lap dances with Angel, a newbie who was rumored to be undercharging and breaking the rules in the VIP room. Lap dances by design are supposed to be anti-climactic. A rule that

Georgia had never broken herself but may have bent a time or two. Still, she resented the competition of the strippers who, mostly the new generation, made the exception the rule. She had no problem with consensual full-service sex work, as long as it stayed out of the club where it wouldn't fuck with her money. Angel was nothing more than a hooker in stripper's clothing.

The cheeseburger burned a hole in her stomach. She couldn't decide whether it was better or worse that a belly full of squirming maggots. She texted Pete that it was ok, *it wasn't, not at all*, and that she hoped to see him soon, *she didn't think she would* and added a smiley emoji with a kissy face. In her head, she told him to fuck off.

She tucked her hair into a plastic cap and hopped in the shower. She didn't usually work Wednesday nights, which meant she wouldn't have any regulars. But she didn't have anywhere close to enough to make her rent in her checking account, or in her safe for that matter. She was simultaneously grateful for the freedom to take on an extra shift, and resentful of not having a steady paycheck. A quick run through with the curling iron, and fresh coat of makeup and she was ready. Or she would be once the energy drink and antacids kicked in. She tossed down a couple of preemptive Tylenol for good measure and headed for the club.

Georgia had to circle the lot for a space, but she wasn't irritated. The lot guy wouldn't be expecting her and so wouldn't have known to put a cone in her regular spot. But he saw her pull in and met her at her car.

Nate the lot guy opened the door for her at the entrance and said, "Hey, sorry girl, I didn't know you were coming in tonight."

"No worries, me either. Something came up and I had to come in."

"I heard that, have a good night."

She nodded at him and stepped inside. Acclimating to the loud music and the dim lighting almost immediately, but it took a few more minutes for the musty odor of old cigarettes and cheap perfume to fade into the background. She spotted her least favorite manager at the bar. Jake was one of the reasons she didn't work Wednesday nights. A malignant narcissist who loved to stir up shit and watch the drama unfold around him, he smiled and waved for her to stop as she tried to scurry past him. She tried on her first of many fake smiles of the shift.

"Hey there, this isn't your usual night," he said his too white teeth glowed under slick backed black hair.

No shit Sherlock.

"Oh yeah, thought I'd give it a try."

"I thought you'd heard."

"No, I guess not. What's up?"

His tone and face were stone.

"Entertainers over forty are now only allowed to work the day shifts. Straight from the owner. But I can give you a couple of stage fee vouchers because I like you. You're a real OG."

Fucking liar. The stage fee voucher wasn't an offer of kindness, but one meant to demean her further while making himself look like the knight in shining polyester. She didn't believe him. This rumor had been going on for six months. Much like the ongoing and tired old rumor of an entertainer purge. This was his schtick. Drum up the fear of being fired or losing shifts. It served his ego well, girls would come and beg for his help to avoid either, thinking he held more leverage than he did. He garnered many favors from the most naïve of the girls. Georgia had never been accused of being naïve, and she wasn't prone to giving favors to douchebags.

She locked eyes with him and called his bluff.

"Oh wow. Huh?"

He reached behind him to a stack of papers and handed her one. It stated exactly what he said and was on the club letterhead. "Sorry, you'll do great on day shift. You're one of our best." His cheesy smile made her cheeseburger want to make a reappearance. "Also, your locker has been reassigned. But I can put you on a wait list for another one. We're going to need you to clear it out."

"Ok, thanks," her fake smile faltered as rage bubbled up from her gut. She caught herself and recovered her smile, but it clashed with the daggers shooting from her eyes.

She took the memo to the DJ booth next to the door of the dressing room. Eric sat on the little stool in front of the sound board. He was also a part-time manager, and likely her only hope to maintain her shifts. She liked him, and he liked her back. Jake was higher up on the management list, but Eric still had some pull. As all strip club DJ's, Eric managed from the shadows. Technically no authority, but with his finger on the pulse of what went on, not much happened without his having a say in it.

"Say hello to our very own hard rocking, hard body Rayna!" Eric put down the mic, "What are you doing here?"

"Need my rent. Is this true?" She held up the memo.

"Yeah, they finally did it. There's a meeting tomorrow, I can put in a word for you, but not sure it will help. Jake's been pushing hard for it, and with the influx of new girls, the nights are getting crowded. Fresh prey for him, I'm afraid. I'm sorry. It sucks, these new girls are a bunch of stupid little twats. You know I'd always rather have OG's" She didn't doubt him, Eric always spoke the truth, even if it wasn't nice. And in the strip club the truth almost never was.

"Fuck. Lost my locker too."

"That was probably Jake. That I can probably work out for you though. But I can't put you on the set list tonight though, I'm so sorry," his words glistened with genuine disappointment.

She squeezed his shoulder, "Thanks. Not sure I can handle the day shift. I don't know what I'm going to do." She didn't have to explain further. Eric knew as well as she did that she could handle a day shift. Twenty-five years as a stripper, there wasn't much she couldn't handle. But being officially put out to pasture, she couldn't handle.

Day shifts at the strip club, at least this strip club, were the death row of aging strippers. The point of no return. They were slow, but also consisted mostly of men on fixed incomes who were either looking for a deal on lap dances or cheap prostitutes. The thought of working that shift turned her guts into knots. A quarter of a decade in a profession that is the epitome of a dead-end job. She had nowhere to go but down. Figurately and literally. She wouldn't retire with a pension, no gold watch, nothing. Her income would only diminish until it disappeared entirely.

"Fuck," she said as she stepped down from the DJ booth. Eric mouthed the words *I'm sorry,* before he spoke into the mic. He was genuinely sorry, and that sucked worse.

She picked up her head, threw her shoulders back, and walked into the dressing room. Walking to her locker she gave the nod to several dancers she was cool with. To call them friends would be a bit of a misnomer. It was hard to make real friends with people you were competing with for money. Allies maybe. But only until the bills were due and money scarce.

She opened her locker. The scent of her own cheap perfume wafted out. She took the bag that hung on the hook at the top out and began to fill it with the contents. Two pairs of cheap plastic platform shoes, three bikinis and a bra and panties set, her cinnamon gum, body spray and deodorant were all the gear she needed, but as she dropped the last item into her duffle bag, she paused. Then put everything back in her locker. Let Jake empty it out. Refusing to suffer both indignities at once. She didn't see any other choice but to come back the next day and take the small pathetic win of keeping her locker. Eric could pull that off, she was sure. She closed the locker, ignoring the sympathetic but predatory looks from the girls as she walked out. Fucking sharks. Not one of them would be sorry to see her go. Allies or not. She kept her eyes straight in front of her, not making eye contact, but not hiding either. She looked right through them and their pseudo-pity.

The road in front of her swam. Day shift would start at noon. The only other club in town would require her to audition. She didn't know what the bigger humiliation would be. Getting rejected by a new club or being forced to work the day shift because of her age. The maggots stirred again, threatening a full-scale riot as she pulled into her space at her apartment. She managed to get the door open before she resurrected her fast food onto the asphalt. *Look at all those undigested calories.* She wiped her mouth on her sleeve, pulled her phone out of her pocket and texted Pete.

Hey, it looks like I can't go back to Cherry's. And it also looks like I will have to move. I have a place to go. Do you think you can help with a mover? Please. I don't know what else to do.

She had enough cash for a mover, and probably enough for living expenses for a while if she didn't have to pay rent. But it wasn't like she would be getting severance pay. Georgia intended to get every last drop of milk from this cow.

Her phone dinged. *I'm sorry. Angel told me about the new rule. I didn't think it would mean you though. You're so gorgeous.*

She resented the compliment, cause fuck him. Angel wouldn't have to worry about the new rule for another decade. The sound of a cash register came from her phone, indicating a deposit was made into one of her pay apps.

Thank you smiling face, praying hands, kissy face emoji's she texted.

That's all I can do right now, Pete responded. Right now, likely meant forever.

Georgia wasn't going to go back to Cherry's Gentleman's club. Not Thursday day shift, or ever. They could cut the fucking lock off her locker and put her shit in the lost and found. Her knees didn't scream at her as she walked up the stairs to not-her-apartment anymore. So at least the Tylenol had kicked in.

5

SHE SAT on the back porch and listened for the sound of crunching gravel from the moving truck. Ralph sat in her lap. She expected to walk into the scent of cat box, or more accurately cat shit. But that hadn't happened. She had left the mangy bastard alone for almost three days, and the sand stayed untouched. The food dish was licked clean though. Georgia gave the house another thorough inspection but hadn't found any place where the thing could've gone in or out from. As if he were nothing more than an apparition moving effortlessly through walls. She had expected her father's house to be creepy, a safe harbor for ghosts. Definitely not the newly renovated and immaculate, borderline charming place it was. Georgia thought the whole idea of ghosts was stupid. Dead is dead. Ralph, and his missing poos remained a mystery. But she didn't feel the need to play Nancy Drew and hunt down the answer. On her list of current priorities, the cat not shitting in the house she was about to sell was all the way down on the bottom.

With her eyes closed, and nothing but the cool fresh air and the sound of birds chirping in the trees, she could pretend she was somewhere else. The town she loathed fell away. She was alone, sort of. Ralph had begun to snore on her thighs, in a new place, with a new life. Her old apartment was just an hour away, but far enough to feel like it was in another time zone. One where all the doors were once again open to her, where she was free to chase the dreams that couldn't be dissolved by strobe lights and a fog machine. The sound she had been waiting for broke her spell.

"Sorry dude," she said to what she thought of her temporary cat. She figured she could find him a new home, when she found her own. Until then, they were partners in crime. Comrades in limbo. She picked him up and set him down on the deck. He followed her inside, but only as far as the front door where he stopped and waited when she stepped outside. Not unlike a ghost bound to its haunt. Apparently even just the front step was past his self-imposed boundary.

The guy driving the moving truck was hot. Like crazy, stupid hot. His passenger not so much. Georgia tucked her shoulders back and looked at the fair-haired hunk with the cut off sleeves, from under her eyelashes. The driver didn't seem to notice.

"Are you Georgia Duran?" The hot guy asked.

"I am."

"Great, I'm Tyler and this is Joe." Joe raised a plump hand in a wave without looking at her.

"Cool. Let me show you inside." Ralph was no longer sitting by the front door. "Do you guys want anything to drink? Water, soda?" She tried her eyelash trick again and looked at Tyler, "Beer?" Her effort at flirting didn't seem to faze him.

"No thanks, Ma'am. We're on a pretty tight schedule. We'll get this stuff unloaded for you right away." Ma'am? She couldn't remember if she'd ever been called Ma'am. She hated it. Tyler opened his mouth, then snapped it shut, before speaking, "Did you just buy this house?" He asked looking at her directly for the first time.

"Not quite," she said thinking hiring a local moving company might have been a bad idea. "It was my dad's. I didn't know him very well. I'm only staying here until it sells."

"Oh, that's good," he said ambiguously. She wanted to ask him what the fuck he meant. Good her dad was dead? Good she didn't know him? Good she wasn't staying long? Or maybe she was being paranoid, and he simply meant 'Good, you got a free house'. Which in its own way was kinda fucked up. She decided that she probably shouldn't care. She also decided he wasn't nearly as hot as she had first thought. She didn't speak to either of them as they unloaded her things and set up her furniture. She dismissed them with an envelope of cash when they had finished, avoiding eye contact and discouraging any more conversation.

After a small meal of brown rice, a meatless veggie patty, and even more veggies, Georgia went back to her small porch with a glass of wine and pre-rolled joint she had picked up at the only establishment in Blackberry Ridge Georgia really cared for. As she touched the tip of it with her lighter, she wondered when the dispensary had opened. And if it would have mitigated her distain for the place. She thought not as she inhaled. They were like Starbucks now, one on every corner. Its addition to the town was just a cherry on a shit sundae.

Ralph appeared again to perch on her lap and to stare at the birds with malintent. She wondered just how many of their kind he had disemboweled. Probably quite a few in the time between her dad dying and him scaring the living shit out of her. Enough to keep him from completely starving to death. Ralph was growing on her though, and the thought of dropping him at a shelter was starting to become more unappealing. She snuffed out the doobie and scratched between his ears.

Her thoughts drifted to where she would move to. Did she want to rent, or would she make enough from the sale to buy her own house? Ralph would complicate renting, as would her lack of employment. And her anemic resume would complicate employment. An unwelcome vision of living in this place permanently bubbled up from the back of her brain. She laughed out loud, "No fucking way." Ralph stopped purring and pinned his ears back for a moment, before resuming his motor.

The sunset was an irritatingly beautiful watercolor of reds and oranges with a smear of yellow behind a darkened tree line. The birds traded places with the country bats as the sun disappeared. She hadn't unpacked much. There didn't seem a point in it. Although the realtor she had hired didn't have high expectations on the house selling quickly. She refused to think that it would take long. Thanks to Pete, she had enough resources to last a few months now that the rent on her apartment was no longer a thing. And that would be more than enough. Her hopes of selling the house quickly to him dissipated. That door was closed. But possibly not locked. She'd lost customers to new girls before. But sometimes they came back. At least she kept telling herself that. Pete is a hard customer to lose. But occasionally, the young ones lacked the skill to hang on to an older customer. It wasn't always about the sexual stuff. Most guys crave intimacy, they want to be seen, understood. And so, sometimes they came back.

Shelley had recommended a realtor who wasn't in town but nearby. She had slipped a business card for Beth Bradley in the large file of paperwork. Their first conversation went well, but there was something that didn't sit right about their second. She had asked if Georgia knew any of the background of the property and sounded surprised when she said she didn't. She heard the voice on the phone take in a breath, as if to ask another question, but then stopped and just confirmed their meeting tomorrow morning.

There had always been rumors about her dad. Eccentric, her mother had called him. As far as Georgia knew, that was simply a euphemism for weird. And apparently, weird was hereditary.

Why her mother and sister were spared, she would never know. But it made Georgia a target. Small towns are known for their sense of community. Their hospitality and looking out for their own. Stereotypes, Georgia had learned were born from ignorance.

The people of Blackberry Ridge were sometimes known as the Berry Folk to the inhabitants of the nearby towns, but they mostly referred to themselves that way. A stupid name that allowed them to conveniently other people that weren't like them. The town was surrounded by and known for its blackberry bushes. They grew wild. Georgia and her sister would pick blackberries in the summer and eat them until they were sick. The dark juice of the berries and the blood from the thorns blended into a macabre liquid that stained the bathroom sink. She loved them as a kid but lost the taste for them when she put her mother and sister into the ground. The gory smears on the imagined faces of the kids who picked these berries now swam in and out of her head. The berries that grew around and maybe up from their graves. Georgia had never, would never consider herself Berry Folk.

Georgia closed her eyes as if it would stop the memories from unearthing themselves. She wasn't the only heavy set, or as her mother called her "big boned" kid in class. But she was the only one that caught shit for it. Every day. She thought if she had any friends, even just one, that it could insolate her. Provide a little shelter from the taunts, the sneers, and the giggles. But the Berry Folk knew as she did that, she wasn't one of them. Never would be. Didn't matter that her mother and Grace had been, or that Georgia herself hadn't picked on anyone. They needed a mark, and she was it. The friend she had hoped for one day had never come. And then, her only people in the world met the front grill of a logging truck. But hey, one of her classmates had told her, at least there's a stop sign there now.

Opening her eyes killed the memory, or at least sent it back where it came from. Not dead, only sleeping.

Her father being so weird didn't help matters of course. The rumors were all bullshit, obviously, but that didn't help. He was uber religious, as many of the Berry Folk, which made the talk of secret gatherings seem even more stupid. He didn't have any friends that she knew of, so who the fuck would even be at his house. Especially late at night. And even more stupid, there was no mention of any cars. What did they think? People hiked in late at night, then hiked out the five miles into the main part of town before morning? No witnesses? Except for the shadows in the windows? No. Theses whispers were as dumb as making fun of her weight. Although, to be fair, her weight was a tangible thing. And if it hadn't been that, it would have been her hair, her clothes, or anything else. A fact proven when a growth spurt hit her freshman year, and she slimmed down to the size people thought she should be. The damage had been done. One of her worst bullies, a tall golden-haired cheerleader, Ann, had come to her one day to apologize. Georgia happily told her to get fucked. She was never going to be one of them. The supposed sightings of his secret rituals and ghosts, or whatever the fuck, were based on nothing, by people whose heads were filled with exactly that. Nothing.

She stood up, then sat back down. Not quite ready to face the night in her temporary bedroom with her temporary cat. Her resentment and memories had quickened her pulse in spite of the wine and the weed. She picked up the joint and lit it again. Determined to blot out her anger. She was an adult, and all these things were as dead as her family. She left the Berry Folk and their so-called community the day her mother and sister died and never looked back.

She snubbed the joint out a second time and walked inside to sleep in the bedroom where her father's body had been found.

Georgia fought her eyelids. The weed and the wine had been useless. Moving usually left her exhausted, but the movers had done all the heavy work. *Thanks, Pete.* Her mind ran in lazy but restless circles. Milky memories of her pubescent years began to surface, only to be pushed under again. Some were pleasant. Most were not. But the pleasant memories were laced with grief. Grief, according to every internet guru, was supposed to get easier with time. Just click bait, Georgia knew now. Grief was a cruel bitch that would never let her go.

Ralph perched at the end of the bed. He tried to snuggle up on her pillow, but as just her temporary cat, this was a bridge to far. He licked her hand to protest her refusal of his pseudo-affection, she knew he was probably just cold, and then fucked off to the foot of her bed. Weighting down the blanket and trapping her feet, not totally uncomfortable, but pushing it. Refusing to acknowledge that she liked not being alone, she wiggled her feet, deliberately disturbing him. Resenting his ability to relax. He picked up his head, then put it back down again. She wiggled her feet.. Ralph simply rode the wave of the blanket. Did she hear him snoring? Enjoying her new game, she slid her foot all the way underneath him and lifted up, wondering just how much he would take before he got up and moved. Determined to win this pissing contest at the end of her bed. Ralph finally relented, stood up and stretched, and jumped to the floor.

Georgia sighed, "There, now maybe I can sleep." Trying to make herself believe her lack of sleep was his fault. She fanned her newly liberated feet out underneath the covers as if to prove her point to herself. She closed her eyes again and began the relaxation technique she had learned from yet another internet guru. This one didn't bother to tell her shit gets easier but offered half-baked coping strategies instead. Preferring bullshit or semi-bullshit solutions to false optimism, she tightened the muscles in her toes, focused on the feeling for a moment, then let go. She moved on to her calf, tightening and letting go. Her knees, she skipped, because of the crackling sound they made when she moved those muscles. The crunchy sound of arthritis.

As she tightened her thighs, she had to redirect her focus. Her mind relaxed enough to wander. A precursor to sleep. Which meant her trick was working. She usually only had to refocus once or twice before she drifted off for good. Or at least a couple of hours before she woke up in a puddle of her own sweat. As she tightened her glutes, a scratching noise, not drifting thoughts disturbed her focus. *Scritch, scritch, scritch.* Squirrels on the roof. Obviously. She tightened the muscles of her ass again, imagining them plump and firm in a pair of yoga pants, she loosened them and breathed out. Hoping she would be asleep well before she got to the top of her head.

Scritch, scritch, scritch.

Fucking squirrels.

Racoons?

She tightened her stomach but released it as she focused on

the sound above her. It sounded closer than the roof. The ceiling?

Scritch, scritch, scritch.

The attic?

Her eyes opened. The attic. Houses out here didn't have basements, but they all had attics. In a house this small they were always just a space between the ceiling and the roof. She must have overlooked the access point. But now, there were rats or squirrels or some other critters up there. She stared at the darkened ceiling, trying not to imagine a body on the floor.

Thump, thump, thump.

Footsteps?

She just stared, trying now not to imagine what was making that noise. Her thoughts returned to the conversation she had with Beth the realtor. *Did Georgia know the background of the house?* Other than her father owned the fucking thing then died in it, so no she didn't know shit about it. Georgia knew she was alluding to the Berry Folk rumors. Secret gatherings, implications of Satanism. And ghosts of course, no rumors of creepy houses and the weird guys who lived there would be complete without a haunting.

Bang, bang, bang.

Georgia was too warm but frozen in her bed, as the ceiling caved in. The fallen drywall held her in place, as the horrific contents of the attic rained down on her. Maggots. Because of course they were. She was pinned to the bed, stunned into silence as her father poured down after the maggots. Not her father, he was dead. His spirit, his ghost, his fucking phantom. The tip of his translucent nose touched hers. His eyes, black holes, his mouth yawned open too widely as he vomited even more maggots. She clamped her mouth shut, wanting to scream but lucid enough to know that no one would hear her. What the fuck could they do anyway? Fuck all. That's what. If this demonic version of her father wanted to kill her, she'd have no chance against him.

The paralysis broke. She was lying in her bed, shivering, sweating. No longer frozen, staring at the intact ceiling. Ralph was back at the end of the bed. His eyes open, staring at her with what in the dark and to her terrified brain appeared to be, but could not have been, concern. An old book she had read came back to her. Old hag. The stories of people being pinned in their beds at night, by an old woman, or man, or demon. Sleep paralysis. A malfunction of the brain that happens on the edge of sleep. Brought on by the sound of squirrels, *squirrels, rats, racoons,* perhaps not on the roof, but in the attic. She listened as her heartbeat began to slow down. But the sound didn't return.

For around half a second Georgia considered resuming her attempt to sleep. But her eyelids wouldn't cooperate, and soon her mind joined in. The realtor is coming in the morning to see the house. The sound of critters fucking around in the attic crawl space was the last thing she needed.

Flinging the covers off her, she swung a naked leg off the side of the bed. A small night light from the bathroom allowed her to find the light switch in the otherwise unfamiliar room. She flicked it on, killing the last malignant shadows in the room.

In her tank top and panties, she began to scan the ceilings. First her father's...Ron's...no... her room. Looking for a break in the freshly painted drywall and a pull or handle. When she didn't find one, she moved on to the hallway, then the second bedroom, hallway, living room and kitchen and back to her bedroom. Her eyes landed on the closet, and she felt like an idiot.

She slid open the closet door and looked up to see exactly what she had been looking for. A four-foot square access hatch with a pull string. She pulled. And gagged. Eat your heart out

Nancy, she had solved the case of the mysteriously missing cat shit.

"What the actual fuck Ralph?"

Ralph didn't answer. Instead, he mewed at her from the floor of the closet. Fully awake now, she pulled down the small ladder that led into the hole in the ceiling. She held her breath as she put her head through the opening.

Expecting to find a few weeks' worth of used cat food, maybe the remains of a dead bird or two, and an unfinished floor lined with inedible cotton candy pink insolation, she found a functional room. Completely furnished. Or mostly furnished. She was immediately grateful that her father was found on the floor of the master bedroom and not on the small twin bed in the attic.

She solved another mystery. Screw Nancy, she was a regular Columbo. The house looked unlived in because it was actually unlived in. That didn't solve all the questions around the house and its makeover. But she didn't really care much.

She blinked to clear her watering eyes and climbed up inside. Unlike the rest of the house, the attic had clearly been lived in. A small dresser sat next to the bed. A dim light burned on top of it. Her father.... Ron.... must have been on his way up here when he keeled over on the floor of the master bedroom. Lucky her. The cat shit was bad, a dead body would be worse. It occurred to her that she had never asked how or by who her father had been found. A neighbor Shelley had said. But what neighbor? A tiny pang of guilt pinged in the depths of her chest. She hadn't asked because she hadn't cared. She scanned her feelings and discovered she still didn't.

The quilt on the little bed was rumpled. Ralph, she assumed. She still hadn't figured out how he was getting in and out, but that information was right under her feet now. Or her nose. The longer she stood in the attic, the more nuanced the stench became. The cat odor was unmistakable, although she didn't see a cat box. But the underlying sweet smell of rot had no obvious origin.

And then it did.

In the far corner of the attic, she spotted a small table and food prep area. She wondered if she could convince Beth, it was a kitchenette? An attic apartment might add to the sale price. Unlikely. The smell would undo any potential value, obviously. Her eyes were leaking, although she had stopped retching.

There was no refrigerator, but there was a small camping stove and pot. A garbage can, filled with banana and clementine peels and an impressive amount of instant ramen wrappers sat next to the little table. So, he hadn't died of scurvy, but she didn't think she could rule out death by sodium. Several pieces of the uneaten fruit appeared to have melted into a black sludge. And that explained the smell. She wondered if maybe she might have a career as a PI in her future. Something to consider at least, she was pretty sure private investigators were self-employed.

Georgia had hit her jump scare limit, so when Ralph unexpectedly brushed against her leg, she didn't think ghost or ax murderer. She reached down to scratch his head.

"Ok, buddy. How have you been coming and going?"

Again, he refused to answer.

Grey light began to creep in through the porthole window close to the little bed. Something was off about this improvised apartment. Other than the fact that Ron had been living here and not in the house. All at once she knew what.

It was smaller than the entirety of the house. The bare walls enclosed a space that allowed for the barest of living. There had to be more. She went to the back wall, which she thought might mark where the hallway and the first bathroom sat. The sheetrock on the inside wore a slightly different texture than walls that lined the perimeter of the house. It closed off this space. A separation. But one that didn't make sense without a door. Was there another access point to that part of the attic, she wondered. She ran her hand on the rough surface and her fingers found an anomaly. Just a slight depression, nearly invisible. She pressed on it, and the wall slid open and into itself. A light clicked on as the door rolled into place as several robed figures reached for her.

Georgia screamed.

7

THE DARK CLAD people didn't move, and she stopped screaming and began to laugh. Fuck Nancy Drew and Columbo, this was some Scooby Doo shit. The scary illusion was proven to be just a silly old man playing a joke. Suddenly the Berry Folk didn't seem quite so crazy. If she had seen a bunch of people in black robes backlit in an attic window, she might have thought the same thing. Secret gatherings, at least it wasn't an orgy. Which had crossed her mind a time or two if she were being honest with herself. A thought far too gross to entertain for any amount of time. But whatever the fuck he was doing up here wasn't with real people, but mannequins. Creepy as fuck, but it ultimately answered another question. And proving again in pure Scooby style, that mysteries don't always have the most sensational causes. Just an old man in a mask.

The smell of cat piss and shit grew stronger, as did the smell of rot. The hidden door was not airtight, it seemed. And if she looked past the mannequins, she saw the overflowing cat box. She fist-bumped one of the robed figures whose arm was outstretched as she walked to the other side of the room, making it wobble. On the opposite sides of the back wall, sat the cat box and a food and water dish. Both dry and clean. But in the middle of the wall lied the answer to what Georgia thought of as the final mystery.

A small cabinet with a wooden door fitted with magnets sat in the middle of the wall, providing separation between the used and unused cat food. Her father was not such a monster as to put the food dish next to the poop box. Ralph stayed close by, a trooper by any standard, as her scream should have sent him running. He nosed the door on the cabinet, custom by the look of it, and it opened to a dark space, she assumed must lead to the house below. A tunnel or corridor, definitely big enough for a cat, maybe even a small human. If her orientation was accurate, she thought it might lead to the pantry in the kitchen. The door to which was on springy hinges that didn't lock. It would easily open with the nose of a determined feline. The magnets clicked it closed when he stepped back. Ralph had answered her after all.

Next to the water and food dishes sat an empty bag of cat food. A small one. Ralph must have helped himself, as the corner of it had been chewed through. She still thought he must have also dined on a bird or perhaps a mouse or two, as even a full the bag couldn't have lasted him very long. She turned to leave, intending to get a bag to dump the garbage and rotting food before the Realtor showed up in…..

Fuck. The grey morning light coming in through the only window had turned yellow. The night had slipped away.

As she turned to leave, thinking she would clean up the garbage and cat box and deal with the rest later, she saw a large closet door. This must be where all his missing things would be. She didn't want to open it. But it's not like she could avoid it. She would need to figure out how to dump all the crap up here. The closet ran the length of the wall, and had a sliding door, it didn't appear to be too deep, and she had a fleeting hope that logistically it couldn't hold that much stuff. The door stood open a few inches and as she reached to push it open, more of that sickly-sweet odor lurched out. More rotting fruit.

Instead, she found more mannequins. No. Halloween decorations. A grinning skeleton, a disturbingly real-looking rotting zombie complete with gnaw marks on its calves and loops of glistening intestines hanging out of a jagged hole in the abdomen. Its throat gaped open. Surprisingly no rotting food, at least that she could see. She had been expecting meat of some sort. But the odor persisted. Was stronger actually.

She stared at the skeleton. One so realistic it must have been expensive. Same with the zombie, and despite knowing better, she thought seemed to be the source of the smell. Flies she hadn't noticed before began to drift out of the closet. Ralph wound himself around her legs and creeped into the dark space. When he began to nibble on the shin of the zombie, she tapped him with her toe.

"Dude, don't do that."

For once he listened, and stopped, but not before emitting an irritated mew.

Something squirmed in her stomach. Were the butterflies back?

No.

A lone maggot wriggled its way out of the zombie's eye socket and dropped to the floor. And she was unable to fool herself anymore.

There were points in her career as an exotic dancer where she really needed to not be completely connected to the moment. A well-paying customer with breath that smelled like he had just finished eating rotten fish out of a dog's asshole. Perhaps one whose grip was tight to the point of pain but had a pocket full of hundreds and a head full of Jack Daniels.

Customers who toed the line but kept buying. She had learned, inadvertently, to disassociate. Her mind stayed just in touch enough to stay physically in control, but not completely there. Like someone grabbing her tit through a push up bra. There was a vague sensation, but not quite a violation. Her mind would drift to a place where she wasn't counting the seconds, or each beat in the song, until the dance was over. It wasn't something she did consciously at first, although once she understood she could do it and how, she could slip in and out at will. Simply put her body on autopilot.

She did that now.

Georgia closed the door. She moved past the figures in the room, and not checking to see if Ralph were behind her, closed the secret door. She dropped down the access point, putting one foot on carefully on the ladder. Her foot planted wonky, and her foot wobbled, threatening to collapse. She slowly let out her breath and replanted her foot. She closed the door in the ceiling and then the closet door.

Her phone was sitting by her bed. She checked the time. It was six a.m. Two hours until Beth showed up. She agreed to the early time, because she was in a hurry to be done with all this. Every hour not spent selling the place was an hour wasted. She now regretted that impatience. She called Beth. She would cancel the appointment. No big deal. But would definitely need to reschedule. She got the voicemail, and she spoke, quickly but calmly and with no clue what was going to come out of her mouth.

"Hello, Beth. I'm sorry to call so early, and to have to cancel on such short notice, but I woke up not feeling well this morning." She paused, realizing she sounded like she felt just fine. She added a slight husky veil to her voice, then spoke again, "I have a fever. I think it best if we reschedule." She hung up, with a breath of relief.

Now she could focus on the problem. She took a glass of

water out to the porch. Georgia thought she would skip the coffee this morning. She was planning on sipping a cup out on the porch. She didn't like the town, but she appreciated the quiet nature of the place. The un-urbanized beauty of the scene. It wasn't the birds and the deer's fault, the town sucked. The adrenaline surging through her body was an unwelcome but effective substitution for the caffeine.

She stared out into the raw land behind her father's house, she again had to tell herself that it was hers. That was her property out there. Her land. She hadn't actually walked those grounds in decades. And not much even then. The house sat on two acres that backed up to public land. She had begged once to walk the trails on the other side of the fences. Thin dirt paths that snaked in and out of the wild bushes and trees. She and Grace wanted to explore so badly. Both her father and mother were adamant. They were not to go anywhere near them. Those were not real trails, but deer, coyote, or even mountain lion or bear trails. She couldn't see the end of the property from where she sat. She wondered again what might be out there. Animals and forest and raw land. Bones?

She pulled her mind out of the forest. She had let it drift, but it had given her body time to adjust to the shock. She sipped her water. She had begun to shiver. She needed to call the police. It would fuck up everything. Like everything. But that was the only thing to do. There are bodies in the house. She didn't kill them, and she wasn't in the business of disposing of human remains. Any remains for that matter. She was hesitating. Who knew how long it would take to deal with this, and would it effect the sale? This opportunity, good fortune to have come into a piece of property as she aged out of her job, had turned into a nightmare overnight. But she was dealing with human life. Lives. These people, or their families, deserved if not justice, to know what had happened. To be put to rest with dignity. Not to be chewed on by a mangy cat. Even if they were Berry Folk. Ralph had followed her out and had fallen asleep on the chair. She looked at him resenting his oblivious calm. She pulled her phone out of her back pocket and stared. Wondering if she really could just empty the attic. There was a burn barrel sitting in a clear patch of the back yard. Where her father had burned trash and yard trimmings. Did bone burn?

She looked at her phone again, she had to call. She wasn't going to burn any bodies. She was being ridiculous, and she knew it. She wasn't that person. An asshole occasionally, but she wasn't the kind of person to desecrate human remains for her own convenience. But still she stared at the phone. Hating the thought of the police out here, the looks she would get in town. The looks she would get from the cops. She was not a criminal, and never had been. A pot smoker before it was legal, sure. Maybe she had snuck an item out of the grocery store, and the IRS might like to have a word, but burning bodies to cover a crime? No. That was not her. She opened the screen on her phone and pressed the button to bring up the keypad.

The sound of tires on rocks stopped her. The time on her phone said quarter after seven. Too early for the realtor, but who else could it be? She looked down and saw she was still in her tank top and panties. But that might be appropriate, since she had told the bitch not to come and she was sick. She trotted inside and to the front door just in time to hear the doorbell.

"Hello?" she said through the door, after all she had a fever and could be contagious.

"Georgia? So sorry to come early, I was in the area and thought…."

"I'm sick. I left a voicemail," she replied. She needed to call the police, but she sure wasn't going to do it with Beth at the door.

"Oh, sorry I didn't see it. Reception is awful up here."

"Yeah, not a good time, I have a fever. Can you come back?"

Georgia had no intention of having her come back anymore, but it sounded good for now.

"I'm not afraid, I have a mask in the car. I was hoping we could catch up too," she was shouting through the closed door.

Catch up? Georgia was confused.

"I'm sorry, what?"

"It's been so long…" Beth stopped when Georgia opened the door.

Ann Bradley. *Ann Fucking Bradley*. Because of course it was. Beth Bradley read the listing when she called the number on the card Shelley gave her. Bradley, a common enough name.

"Ann?"

"Yeah, Beth is my middle name. Well Elizabeth. I stopped using Ann…." She crinkled her nose, "right after high school."

Georgia just stared at her. Beth looked down at her panties and bare legs.

"Uh, I really feel terrible. Can you come back another day?"

Like never.

"Sure, it's just I'm already here…." She trailed off again, her nose crinkled again. "What is that odor?"

Death, Ann. It's Death.

And cat shit. That too.

A look of disgust bled through the heavy pancake make-up Ann-now-Beth wore. Her platinum hair held in place by a sparkly hair tie that she must have saved from the days of picking on the fat kid in middle school. Why couldn't she get away from these people?

"You know, I should probably come back another time. I don't know what you have going on here. But it reeks in there." The disgust intensified. "I should have known you'd have ended up like him. I don't know why I agreed to work with you."

Georgia knew, an easy commission. She knew who Georgia was, the moment they first spoke on the phone. A scene from Blackberry Ridge Elementary of Ann and two of her minions blurred her vision. The day they caught her in the gym bathroom.

"You don't know shit," Georgia was becoming angry.

"I know this place is fucking haunted. I know that your daddy was a psycho. I know that you are a whore, so does everyone else."

She wasn't sure if it was the stress of the two bodies in the attic, losing her job, maybe just the lack of sleep, but Georgia didn't know she was going to hit her. Until she did.

Her fist shot out as if disconnected from her body. She watched helplessly as it connected with Ann's smug face. Her nose to be exact. It flattened under her knuckles, bracketed by wide black lined eyeballs as surprised by the punch as Georgia was.

Beth stumbled backward. Her head landing on the crack in the walkway, Georgia never stepped on as a kid. *Step on a crack, break your mother's back.* Her skull made a terrible sound, her eyes stayed wide, staring at nothing. Georgia took a step forward, intending to help her up, but paused instead. Just staring. Blood poured out beneath the blond bob cut and from her nose. Her ice blue eyes didn't blink.

Georgia shook her head to clear the not totally unwelcome vision. She felt a stinging in her fist. She had never hit anyone before. Not all the years of constant bullying and cruelty. She wondered if this first punch was thirty years too late. If she had punched her that day in the bathroom maybe that would have made it stop. But she didn't. When the three girls busted the lock on the stall. Georgia had been grateful she had already pulled up her pants when they grabbed her. They yanked on her clothes, pulling her shirt over her head and knocking her to the floor. She didn't remember the words they were chanting. Just the chanting. Just the kicks to her belly. They had run themselves to the school office, screaming self-defense, leaving Georgia crying on the floor. Georgia was threatening us. She hit us, we had to get away. Ann Elizabeth Bradley could do no wrong. Had never gotten in trouble, straight A's popular, slim, and pretty. Georgia chubby, quiet and moody, and from such a weird family. She never had a chance. She was suspended and reprimanded. Her mother talked to the principal, but it was three girls' words against her.

Georgia smiled.

8

GEORGIA WASN'T the kind of person to destroy human remains. Until she was. After she dragged Ann's body to its car, coincidentally, a black BMW, but four years older than her own, she retrieved Ann's phone from the sink full of water it had been sitting in and slipped it in the dead woman's pocket. The cell service out here was spotty at best. The nearest cell phone tower was miles away. She hoped it the last time this phone pinged, whoever was looking wouldn't be able to tell if it was at Georgia's house, or the pond in which they would find the realtor and her car. Georgia didn't know much about cell towers and the like, but she had once sat in the lap of a telecom engineer who liked to talk.

She didn't remember making the decision. She just started to do it. She propped Ann in the passenger seat and drove the car down the road to the large pond. The one she had always wanted her dad to take her fishing at. She drove around to the back side, the side where the access to the pond was steep and crawling with thorned black berry bushes. She wrestled the body to the driver's side; it was much easier than she had thought. She wedged the knock off shoe down on the luxury car's gas pedal. She released the brake, and the car bumped down the hill and into the water. Almost gliding on the surface, a blasphemous mockery of the messiah walking on water. Ann Bradley, deified.

Georgia didn't breathe as she watched the car sink far too slowly, thinking it might just float there. But the murky water soon filled the cabin, washing away the blood on the passenger seat. The wound on the back of the head was small. Just a little crack. The nose could have easily been broken by the steering wheel. Assuming that the fishies hadn't nibbled it off by the time the body was recovered. If it was recovered. No houses lined the road to the pond from her father's house. Sure, as shit, there were no cameras out here. The Berry Folk were private, they minded their own business. Unless of course there was more interesting business to mind.

Georgia stood in her tank top and panties at the edge of the pond. Barefoot. The half mile walk back would tear up her feet. The road wasn't much of a road back up in here. Just gravel. Not even well-worn gravel. This wasn't a place people went often, and the rocks that covered the dirt didn't get much opportunity to see any tires at all. Blackberry bushes that lined the road back here still had months before little hands would come to pick their fruit.

The walk back did tear up her feet, but Georgia didn't feel it. She didn't jog but walked fast and was safe, or safe-ish back in her home in ten minutes. From start to finish the whole thing took less than an hour. Her mind conjured up a real estate ad. "Come to Blackberry Ridge, where the bodies disappear in a jiffy."

Ralph was staring at her when she woke up. The dream of disposing of Ann's body had felt so real, it left the lingering stink of guilt, the guilt that rushed back to her after Ann-not-Beth slouched toward her car, holding her bloody nose, and drove off yesterday. But there was still a large part of her that wished she had the balls to have actually killed the sour old bitch and dumped her in the pond. But at least she had the memory of punching her in the face. Something she had had coming for the last twenty-five years. The fucking nerve of Ann to think that she would want to work with her in any capacity.

Sitting on her bed as if there were no bodies in the attic. Her top sheet was soaked with sweat, as if she had taken a dip in the pond herself. She got in the shower, letting the hot water wash away the dream of the body in the pond. Her mind fuzzed with thoughts that wouldn't completely materialize. The rest of the day after a bleeding Ann Bradley fucked off, went by in a haze, waiting for the police to show up and arrest her for assault. When she finally crashed and burned, she did it in her bed and not the county jail. Maybe Ann didn't call the police because she felt bad about all the bullying. Georgia drowned that thought before it had a chance to take hold.

Now that she had breached the seal to the attic, the uncontained stench leaked through the ceiling. Morning had arrived with false happiness on a ray of sunshine. She opened every window in the house. Whoever was up in the attic had been there for a while. She couldn't help them, and they could only get her in trouble. Georgia pulled out her phone, the battery was low. Georgia set her phone to charge. She fished some old jeans and a stained t-shirt of a moving bin and pulled them on.

This would be the point where someone might call a friend. Calling the police was no longer an option, but if she were honest with herself, it had never really been one. Not a good one anyway. A ride or die, is what she needed. The one person who promised to help hide a body over a rum and coke at a karaoke bar. Georgia ran over the list of potential friends in her head. She practiced what she might say to them. *Hey, I need some help getting rid of some trash.* Or maybe, *so funny thing. I got two dead people in my new house.* She wasn't going to call anyone.

Georgia valued her independence. The kind of independence that didn't lend itself to close relationships. She was reaping what she sowed. She had no ride or die. She had Ralph.

One cup of coffee down, she trekked out to the detached garage. Ron's little pickup truck sat on near flat tires on the dirt floor. It was too dark to tell the color of the truck, somewhere between shit brown and puke green. The dusty work bench held an impressive collection of tools. She wasn't sure where to start, so she just started. She picked up a hammer and lightly smashed it onto a pair of work gloves. Squishing the real or imaginary spider hiding in them. She pulled them over her hands and let her breath out when she didn't feel any spider goop. So far, so good. Baby steps. Don't think, just do.

The house sat on two acres. Most of it trees and closely cropped weeds that aspired to be grass. Birds chirped a happy, "It's a wonderful day to dispose of your father's murder victims" song. The coffee burned in her brain, danced with her exhausted thoughts, and almost made her want to sing along with them. Stress induced delirium wasn't all bad. The houses nearby wouldn't hear her in any case.

Gloves on, she surveyed the contents of the small dark garage. A string with a little metal bobble brushed her nose and she pulled on it. A dirty bulb made the garage light up. Sort of. The glow burned through a thick layer of dirt. But it was enough to see a large cardboard box of sturdy black plastic bags. The box showed a picture of discarded building materials, branches and other sturdy garbage. Contractor bags. Conveniently, the bags sat next to a hacksaw. She smiled. It was like it was left just for her. A brief flicker of the reality of the situation tried to harsh her mellow, but she wouldn't let it. A few hours of work, and the attic would be empty, or at least devoid of human and food remains, and she could rest. Maybe on the sofa, maybe she could even figure out how to get something to watch on the TV she hadn't yet plugged in.

She left the light burning, her sneakered toe hit a bag full of something hard close to the door. Lime. Because of course. A staple of the creepy satanic murderer. Bags and hacksaw in hand, she stepped back out to yard and the birds stopped singing. The sunlight refused to be silenced, and it sang in her eyes and made them water.

Ralph sat at the back door, ready to help. Or supervise. Her ride or die. She had no intention of taking him anywhere now. She checked her phone, mid-morning. She had a bag of cloth face masks stored in a plastic baggie, thinking that if only the girls that had been driven online during the pandemic had stayed there and not come back to the club, she might still have a few good years left in her as a stripper. Her knee buckled, and she remembered that was bullshit. She was done. She was clearly moving into a new era of her life. One filled with excitement. And dead bodies. And cat shit. She layered two masks and secured them behind her ears.

Her eyes watered again as she opened the access door in the ceiling of the closet. Ralph met her as she climbed up. Quickly she prioritized her tasks. One. Bodies. Two. Cat box. Three. Rotten food. The mannequins watched her as she opened the closet door. The skeleton was fairly easy. She didn't even need the saw. It was like taking apart a puzzle. Or a Halloween decoration. When each piece had been placed in the bag, she found she still had room for more.

She yanked the other body out and found it to be a bit trickier. But still not that bad. Relatively speaking. She had discovered a new use for her stripper neurosis. Dissociation reimagined. Georgia sawed off the head, the limbs, and left the trunk intact. The saw bit through the deteriorated flesh easily. She fit all of it into the bag with the other bones and put the saw on top of all of it. She dragged it to the access hatch and stuffed it down. She cringed not knowing what it would sound like as it hit the floor. It landed with an unceremonious thump. Just a bag of old clothes.

Georgia retched not at the overflowing cat box, but the rotten food. It all went into a bag too. The worst was over. Almost. Both bags of foulness were out of the attic, and soon out of the house too. She set them both by the burn pile. Back in the shed she found a large bottle of disinfectant cleaner and brushes and rags. On her way back to the attic, she grabbed her phone and portable speaker. Metal blaring, she cleaned the melted remains of the food and the Halloween decorations. A sense of normalcy seeped into her mind. A breeze forced its way through the window in the attic and soon she could remove her mask. Things were looking up.

Her phone buzzed. A text. Eric.

Hey girl. How ya doing?

She smiled, then frowned. It wasn't only strippers that dealt with the stigma of working in the sex industry. The male staff caught plenty of shit too. Another stereotype born of baseless assumptions. For every Jake, there were two or three Erics. She took off her gloves and texted back.

I think I'm ok. Cleaning out the attic of my house. I'm not coming back btw.

The reply came quickly.

I figured. It sucks here anyway. Been slow as fuck. New girls undercharging, overperforming, and undertipping. Thought you'd like to know, Angel got fired. Got caught stealing.

He was right. She did want to know. Stealing was a cardinal sin of the strip club. For all the cattiness and backstabbing competition, stealing was unforgiveable. The strip club bore a community bound by stigma. There were certain lines that just weren't crossed. Stealing was one of them.

I love that for her. Smiling love face.

Good luck girl. Stay in touch. Miss you like crazy.

Georgia didn't think she just typed, regretting hitting send right after she did.

You should come up here and see my new place. Fuck.

I would love that. Came his immediate reply.

She and Eric had a bit of a thing. An unacknowledged, don't shit where you eat kind of thing. She liked the way his eyes roamed her body. It was obvious, but unintrusive. Suggestive, but not disrespectful. Their decade long flirtatious banter had led to nothing, but she wondered now. Ridiculous as it was, maybe it didn't have to be nothing. Fuck it. She texted him the address.

9

THERE WERE no nightmares on her third night in the room where Ron died. She woke up refreshed and feeling positive. Perhaps a symptom of perimenopause. Mood swings don't always have to go down. Whatever the cause, Georgia smiled.

Country sunlight blasted unfiltered through curtainless windows, annoying Ralph. It was Friday, the day the shelter opened. But Ralph was going nowhere. He'd probably rip her to shreds if she tried to take him out of the house anyway. She had set the coffee pot the night before and she heard it gurgling its last bit of manic darkness into the pot. Eric was coming today. Over the last decade or so, she strangled the romantic thoughts of him as soon as they emerged. She wasn't any kind of romantic. Romcoms made her want to jump in front of a bus. Love was simply a chemical reaction. Her entire career, if you could call stripping a career, centered around creating an emotional and physical reaction based on a flimsy fantasy. She knew she wasn't immune to being fooled by her own brain, but for the moment she was enjoying the feeling. Life is short, death unescapable. Georgia wasn't going to let a good feeling go unappreciated. There was no telling how many good feelings she had left to feel before her own body gave up for good.

She got up, further annoying Ralph, who hunkered down farther into the covers. She walked into the kitchen, where the windows were also curtainless. But her neighbors would need binoculars to see her, and so what if they did? After twenty-five years dancing naked, anyone who hadn't seen her tits by now would be the anomaly. They would be far more special if they hadn't seen her naked. In her apartment, she once received a complaint for daring to walk in front of a window naked. Country life had its advantages.

Having rid the attic of the worst of its secrets, she closed off the little tunnel her new buddy had been using. She checked the cat box she had set up in the second bedroom and found it used. She cleaned it, filled his water and food dishes in the kitchen. She opened all the windows again, just in case the funk of rotting food and other things lingered.

Ralph joined her on the back porch and hopped into her lap. She checked her phone. Grateful that the internet sucked out in the middle of nowhere there wasn't much to look at. The coffee began to melt the sleep fog, and her gaze fell to the large black plastic bags sitting by the burn barrel. One full of cat shit and rotted food and the other with...Halloween decorations. She looked away.

A strange peace of mind had replaced the drone like thoughts of the day before. A weird kind of resolve took over. She was here. And will be here for a while. And even if it were only temporary, she wouldn't be alone. Ralph looked up from her lap as if he read her mind and was insulted by her thought. She scratched between his ears.

"You're not all that bad, but it will be nice to have someone that doesn't shit in a box for a little while."

Now that she was going to need a new realtor, Georgia figured she was going to stay for a while. She unpacked some boxes and filled her dresser. She stowed her things and organized her kitchen, she hung a few curtains to blunt the sunlight, and completely missed the knock at the door when it came. When Eric tapped her on the shoulder as she sat on the kitchen floor, she was glad she had already put the knives away. Had she been holding one, she might have stabbed him.

"Settle down there chicky, you look like you just saw a ghost!"

Georgia said nothing but hopped to her bare feet and hugged him. Much too hard.

"Dude, you have no idea how glad I am to see you."

"I bet. I'm happy to be here. Drama has gotten pretty thick. Jake on a power trip. New girls bawling. Cheap customers. Not a country boy, but the drive up here is gorgeous."

"It has its perks. Can I get you something to drink?"

They spent the next hour or so wrapped in sexual tension on her back porch. Without the strobe lights and loud music, the tension turned to honesty. Ralph jumped off her lap when Eric's lips touched hers.

She had always been a fan of the one-night stand. Sometimes even two nights if they weren't in a row. They weren't as easy to come by as one might expect given her job. Guys who weren't totally intimidated by her work, or jealous, didn't exist in large numbers. So, her romps tended to be few and far between. Maybe once a month or so, guys she met at the bar or other places away from the club. Customers were off limits, even the ones she really liked. And a serious relationship was out of the question. As a little girl, Georgia didn't dream of a large wedding and an SUV with a back seat full of crotch goblins. She had a bucket list that had grown long but maybe not completely unobtainable. She hadn't ruled out a partner, but she wasn't counting on one either. Funny, how one kiss could change so much. Suddenly she had exactly no idea what she wanted. The mistaken encounter with Mike all those years ago, taught her that she could simply enjoy sexual experiences on their own. The who wasn't all that important.

Georgia wasn't upset or offended, but she was a little surprised that he had packed for the weekend. She was also surprised to find that she was afraid that a weekend wouldn't be enough. Her ovaries seemed to be throwing up desperate signs, somehow aware that they would soon be rendered irrelevant. Her reproductive organs were already just for show, if not totally unfunctioning.

They had moved from the back porch to the bedroom. She didn't think he needed to know that they were fucking in the room where her father was found dead. Not a pertinent piece of information. Besides, people died all the time everywhere. There couldn't be many places left on the entire planet where a someone hadn't died at some point in time. Dwelling on such a fact of life was pointless.

After working out a decade of unacknowledged lust. *Love? Puke.* Georgia and Eric were starving. She had stocked up on a few staples at a grocery store in the biggest town nearest Blackberry Ridge on her way up. But things had taken several unexpected turns since then. The store that she had stopped at the edge of the mountain road, was nearly an hour away.

"There must be a grocery store here in town," Eric said. The sight of him lying naked on her bed made her head spin. He was nearly fifty, but the gray in his chest hair gave her goosebumps.

"There is." She paused, wondering just how much he might want to know about her childhood here. "But the town is weird. Bunch of self-righteous assholes."

"So? Fuck them all sideways. There's a grill outside, we'll grab some steaks, and some charcoal, and I'll serve you the best piece of meat you've ever had."

He was baiting her. And she swallowed it whole.

"You already have…." She smiled and kissed him. "Growing up here wasn't awesome, but you're right. Fuck them sideways."

They didn't bother to shower, just got dressed and she drove them into the heart of Blackberry Ridge. They pulled up to the little grocery store, thumping base and dark guitar riffs announcing both their arrival and her unrelenting resentment. Eric took her hand as they walked through the door.

Inside the small grocery shop she was thirteen again. Pudgy and pimpled, she wanted nothing more than to disappear into the walls. She recognized the woman at the counter immediately and gripped Eric's hand. It must have hurt, but he didn't flinch. The woman looked up from a tabloid. The store hadn't changed in decades and the magazine stand still held cheap romance novels and copies of the very worst examples of sensational garbage. Except instead of black and white pictures of Bat Boy on the *World Weekly News*, there were copies of the *Epoch Times*. Not an improvement. At least the *World Weekly News* didn't try that hard to appear to be true.

"Georgia?" The woman said.

Georgia drew her eyebrows together as far as the Botox would allow and pretended to not know the woman's name.

"Um….yes. I'm sorry, you are?" Stacey. Her name was Stacey McPhearson. Homecoming Queen and twat muffin extraordinaire. She screamed aloud in their shared eighth grade English class that Georgia had lice, pointing to a single white fleck in her hair. Mrs. Stewart panicked in response, covered her head with her paper lunch bag and sent her to the office, where it was determined that Georgia had exactly one flake of dandruff and not lice. But the damage was done. Mrs. Stewart could have undone it but chose not to. She could have announced to the class that it was nothing. She could have apologized for overreacting, she could have done something, anything to stop the relentless taunting that came after. She did nothing, but watch, *with glee? Was that glee in her eyes?* The sneers and giggles and the exaggerated parting of the kids as Georgia came back into class, as if she had just been diagnosed with the plague.

"Stacey. You know Homecoming Queen? I'm sure you remember me."

"Oh sure. Yeah." Georgia looked her up and down, taking extra time at the frumpy waistline, and deep crow's feet. "You look so different. Mature," drawing out the last word as an insult. Georgia would have taken it as one.

"Sorry about your father."

"Thanks." Sorry was rapidly becoming yet another meaningless word.

Eric pulled her toward the back of the store where the fruit and vegetables were displayed. Fresh local produce nearly overflowed the counters.

"Wow. Like wow," he said, fondling a perfect tomato.

"I fucking hate this place, but you won't find better veggies. Would you believe that this isn't the best of it? This stuff is just the leftovers from the weekly farmer's market at the park. Almost everything is grown within a few miles of here."

They bagged what they wanted and moved on to the meat counter. Where Eric was equally impressed. They grabbed the rest of what they needed, and Georgia was again face to face with Stacey. She rang up the food, then bagged it. Eric took both bags as they walked toward the door.

"Ahh…what a gentleman," Stacey said. "Hope he pays well."

Georgia opened her mouth, but Eric didn't let her speak, "Fuck you. You fucking twat."

It was at that moment Georgia knew love.

10

THEY DIDN'T TALK on the ride back to her house. They didn't need to. The interaction at the store relayed to him everything she could have said outloud. Ralph watched with desperate eyes as Eric grilled up a steak for himself and a piece of halibut for Georgia along with some vegetables. They sat and ate on the back porch with their plates in their laps, sipping on glasses of wine. Ralph chased flies in front of a bloody sunset.

Eric took their plates inside, he came back with the bottle of wine, now only half full.

"If you're interested, I brought dessert," he reached into his pocket and pulled out a tiny baggie which held two small pills.

"Is that…"

"Molly? Yes. Yes, it is. You down?"

"Holy shit. I haven't done that in ages." She meant a year or two.

"Me either, but I figured what the fuck. Why not? I got it from you know who. It's good."

She knew who. A bouncer. *The* bouncer, who supplied the club with anything and everything, except meth and heroin. Next to stealing, those were the only other things really frowned upon at the club. Those who chose to partake found themselves in an unacknowledged ugly little club. Georgia's rule when it came to drugs or alcohol at the strip club was, if you had to get fucked up to strip, you need to find another job. She wasn't against getting fucked up, but not at work. You can party at the club, or you can hustle. You can't do both. She'd seen far too many girls confuse the two and end up addicted or broke, but most often both.

"Fuck it. Ok. Let's do it."

He handed her one of the pills and they swallowed them with sips of wine after clinking glasses. Pot and wine were the only things she really indulged in. There had been an occasional coke bender with a couple of other strippers she had hung out with. But after a bad comedown that left her hating life and in dire need of a burrito, she decided that blow wasn't for her. An expensive panic attack, but MDMA was fun occasionally.

They sat outside as the sun disappeared along with the wine. She filled up two very large glasses of water when they went inside. Sitting on the sofa, she snuggled up next to Eric. He traced the bare skin on her arm, and she shivered. He picked her up in his arms, laid her on the bed and stripped her. Soon he was naked on the bed with her. They touched, talked and fucked. They touched, talked, and made love. A phrase as dumb as passed away, but she found she didn't mind it just then. It felt right. Everything felt right. Warm, and tingly, and perfect. Contentment. She couldn't be sure how much the drugs intensified her feelings. But she knew they were real and not chemically induced. The drugs simply drew a white hot flame around them.

Then she fucked it all up.

"There are dead bodies out by the burn barrel," Georgia said in low voice, almost a whisper. Her eyes had been closed and her mind drifted in lazy loops and circles as the molly began to wear off. She didn't even realize she had said anything at all until Eric responded.

"Wait what?" His eyes had been closed too, but he opened them when she spoke.

Georgia's head was in the crook of his arm, so her response was muffled, "Uh...I didn't mean to tell you." Her brain still wanted to be lazy, but the realization of what she had just said brought her back into the room and full consciousness. "Fuck."

"Too late, so for real. What the fuck?"

"I found bodies in the attic," she said flatly. "Cat shit too. Like a lot of cat shit."

Eric raised an eyebrow but said nothing.

"My dad...Ron...must have killed them? Or found them and hid them maybe?" Georgia wanted to mitigate her strong suspicion that her father killed them. She was almost sure, but she wanted to hang on to the idea that she could be wrong. "Vagrants or hitchhikers they must have been. And from a while ago, there wasn't much left." Halloween decorations her brain insisted.

He didn't ask why she didn't call the police, "Do you think there are any more?"

"I don't."

Anxiety poked through what had been a pleasantly exhausted calm as she searched his face for a reaction. They were both sitting up and facing each other. Why the fuck had she confessed?

Confessed. Yet another dumb word. Confessed to what? She hadn't done anything wrong. She didn't kill anyone. She struck someone, but she left that part out. Almost more embarrassed by her lack of control than her desecrating human remains. Objective morality, much like objective truth, is a myth. A made-up thing. One could get close maybe, but in the end, morality is as subjective as art or music. One person's truth could easily be someone else's delusion. Morality is a squishy thing. Someone might say she was a criminal; she had committed a crime in getting rid of the bodies. Technically. But she hadn't done anything with malice, did she deserve punishment? Eric didn't think so. Eric didn't blame her. He wanted to help her. He held her as they fell asleep.

The gurgling of the coffee pot set the night before to start brewing at mid-morning woke her up. Her mind told her she should be freaking out, but the lingering drugs kept her calm. She heard faint snoring, Ralph sleeping at the end of the bed. She put a hand on Eric's naked back and felt a rush of fear that he wasn't breathing. Dead. But he was warm to the touch and leaned into her hand with a low contented moan. He turned over to face her.

"Good morning beautiful."

She had read in some silly article that strippers were immune to compliments. A goofy sentiment that rang utterly true. But Eric's compliments infected her to the core. She thought she might be blushing. Her face went pale when she thought of the night before.

"Uh…"

He put a single finger to her lips, "It's ok. We got this. It's me and you baby." Ralph stirred. "And Steve."

She laughed, "It's Ralph."

He made a puking sound, "Oh yeah. Rrraaalllppphhhh."

She kissed him, but they pulled away from each other after only a second.

"Whoa buddy…." She crinkled her nose, "You remember your toothbrush?"

"Look who's talking…."

She socked him in the shoulder.

"Coffee will fix that. Temporarily, at least."

Georgia walked naked to the kitchen and came back with two mugs of coffee. She pulled on the T-shirt Eric had dropped on the floor and he put on his boxers which had also been on the floor. His discarded clothing worn like puzzle pieces. They took the coffee back outside to the porch.

Her head was fuzzy, and her body ached. But in a good way. Her muscle soreness only served to remind her of the way her body had reacted to his. A calm way. A calm she wished was organic but that she knew was likely chemically induced. Dark thoughts laced their way through the peace in her mind.

"What the fuck am I going to do?"

"What the fuck are WE going to do?"

"I'm so sorry to have dragged you into this. This isn't your shit. Just forget I said anything."

"Not a chance." His eyes found hers, "If I think this is what I think it is, then I'm here. For as long as you want me here. George, I never wanted to hope that this could happen, but I think it's happening."

Clunky and awkward, she got it. And she felt it too. A tear snuck out of her eye and slid down her cheek.

"Are you sure? This is some shit."

He shook his head, "Show me the attic."

She took him to the closet where the access door was cut into the ceiling. She tried to go in first, but he stopped her. She watched as his shoes disappeared. She climbed up after him. She closed her eyes as she watched him look at where Don had spent his last days. Or maybe all of his days. The timeline of his life was smeared in a wash of uncertainty, rumors, and lost memories. She thought she should be ashamed. Embarrassed that she shared DNA with this unhinged and mysterious recluse.

"Wow," Eric looked around. Georgia had closed the secret door after she finished cleaning the worst of the mess. She was impressed with her efforts, there was no lingering odor. "There's more. This isn't the whole thing," he said.

She told him about the bodies in the closet but had left out the mannequins the night before. She might have been high, but not high enough to spill all the beans. Maybe ironically, she was much more embarrassed about the fake humans, which had quite obviously borne the rumors of the secret meetings, than she had about the dead people in the attic. The corpses had kind of been the main event in the whole saga anyway. Hanging out with pretend people seemed somehow worse than killing them.

"Yeah, there is. It's really weird though. Like I know the whole thing is weird and fucked up, but it gets weirder." Her voice cracked, and her eyes began to burn with tears. She didn't want to tell him about the rumors of her dad, or the merciless bullying because of it. Her mother and her sister. But the mannequins were the culmination of all that. The proof that the Berry Folk were right. The Berry Folk's justification and vindication. Even if the secret meetings were just dolls. "There's a secret door," she finished with a grimace afraid it might be a bridge too far for him. Even though he had stayed through the bodies in the attic. The creepy ass mannequins might just end this whole trip. He was staring at her.

"It's ok. I tell you what, let's just handle what we have here. Then we'll deal with whatever is behind that wall." He was looking at the wall with the clandestine door.

The tears she had been fighting spilled over. He hugged her and she closed her eyes. But when she opened them, a realization hit her. "How the fuck did he get all this stuff up through this little hole in the ceiling?"

"A tight squeeze for sure. Probably had to spit on it."

Her tears ran away, and she began to laugh.

"Gross. How about maybe not making sex jokes about my dead dad?"

Eric walked over to the little twin bed and began to inspect it. Then whipped off the top cover with the flourish of a magician. "Behold my love! The answer is..." he raised an eyebrow, "IKEA!"

They spent the next couple of hours dismantling the

furniture with an Allen wrench and dropping the pieces down the access point. The thin foam mattress they had to fold up like a taco, but it went through. It wasn't long before the whole room was empty. Devoid of the belongings of the strange hermit, the attic was almost pleasant. She had opened the small little window, and an afternoon breeze rode in on the sunlight.

The attic was clean, or at least one room of it was, but the bedroom beneath it was a mess. Georgia and Eric carried each bit of Ron's strange life out of the house and to the driveway. The pile that sat next to the garage amounted to only a few feet. A pathetic end to a sad existence, their gaze lingered on the pile before retreating to the back porch.

Exhausted from the night before, the sun was hardly down before they showered together and crawled back into Georgia's bed and fell asleep.

11

GEORGIA SLIPPED OUT of bed while Eric was sleeping. The calm sunlight of the morning was blunted by the realization that he had to leave today. She set the coffee to brew and attended to her unintended pet. Ralph wound himself around her legs, she had thought that he would be upset about losing his hiding space below the roof. But he seemed content just to have a living human servant again.

The coffee pot sputtered its final few drops, and she pulled out two mugs from the cabinet. She began to fill one then the other when a cool hand grasped her shoulder. Her arm jerked and coffee poured onto the counter.

"Sorry babe," he said as he handed her a towel. He kissed her neck as she wiped up the counter. She should have been pissed. But she wasn't. She hadn't really been afraid either. She couldn't stop thinking about him leaving, so maybe she was afraid. "Here let me get that." He took the towel from her and finished cleaning up the mess.

"I don't want you to leave," Georgia blurted. Now she *was* pissed, but at herself. She didn't know when she had become so weak, but she wasn't digging her newfound vulnerability.

"Me either. But I have to. Sunday night shift and all. No one is going to cover for me tonight, but Phil has been bugging for extra DJ shifts. I'll get him to cover for me the rest of the week."

She put her head on his shoulder and said nothing.

He finished pouring the coffee and handed her a mug. Ralph followed them to the back porch where they leaned on the railing and looked toward the burn barrel and to the large black plastic bags.

Eric took an audible breath in and said, "Here's what's up. My friend has a truck. I'll bring it up tomorrow and we'll take all the garbage," he nodded to the black plastic bags which could have easily been full of yard trimmings, "to the dump. Easy peasy. Nothing at all weird about that."

"Wouldn't it be better if we just burned it all?"

Eric thought about it, "The furniture might go, but that mattress is just foam, it will melt and stink like nothing else." He frowned, "No one is going to look at bags of garbage. And besides, those bags of trash were here when you got here weren't they? You're just cleaning up the crap. Burning a bunch of fiber board and plastic might look much more suspicious. Although, I'm really just guessing. This is my first ever murder cover up."

She frowned at him, then nodded. He had a point.

He set his coffee down and embraced her. Ralph, sitting on the railing as if he were part of the whole conversation, head bumped Eric then licked the bald patch on the crown of his head.

The sun was rising way too fast for Georgia's liking but there was exactly nothing she could do about it. They took their mugs inside and showered together. Eric packed up his stuff, making a show of leaving his toothbrush. Before he got into his compact Honda, they took a walk around the property. He said he just wanted to get a feel for the land, but Georgia knew that he was looking for any more unexpected fuckery. She was too, she didn't need any more surprises. He kicked up little piles of brush and leaves, finding only dirt underneath. No freshly dug holes, or latent clothing. She kissed him goodbye, and he promised to text her from the DJ booth and be back as soon as he could the next day.

She couldn't bear to watch him drive up the narrow driveway to the road. Instead, she turned her back to him and went back inside where Ralph sat on the stoop. Still unwilling to step foot beyond the front door or back deck. A deep sense of panic began to bubble in her guts. She started to shake, and her vision swam in and out of focus. She leaned on the railing, waiting for the panic to pass. When her head cleared, she went back inside and wondered how she would pass the hours before Eric came back.

Georgia tidied up the house, but there wasn't much to tidy. Most of her belongings, which weren't much, still sat in boxes. She took stock of her supplies in the kitchen and thought a trip to the grocery store, the big one in the next town over might help her pass the time. And she was right.

The drive out of Blackberry Ridge was as gorgeous as it had been on the way in. She let the wind run its fingers through her hair from the sunroof. Inside the store, the bright lights melted away her anxiety. She shopped, and found herself smiling again, in spite of the next and hopefully final nasty tasks she had in front of her. She wasn't alone. She couldn't remember the last time she could truly say that.

She was still smiling when her foot slipped in the mess on the walk up to her front door. The two bags of groceries she had been holding landed on either side of a large glob of red jello covered in grey and black hair. A racoon. *A sacrifice? A curse?* Its head sat on the railing, tongue lolling out of its mouth. Georgia opened her own mouth to scream but found her lungs were empty. She fought the blackness closing in at the edge of her consciousness.

An apple rolled in the mess at her feet and her thoughts turned to the bruises it would have, not the congealing blood that now coated it. She stepped out of the puddle and made it to her front door. Ralph was waiting when her shaking hand holding the key finally found its way into the lock. He meowed in distress. If it hadn't been for the dead black eyes staring from the railing, she might have been able to convince herself that the little fucker had killed it. Cats were homicidal psychopaths, but that wasn't it. It wasn't her silly hormone raddled brain showing her stupid things again either.

Someone left this for her. Berry Folk.

Her thoughts tried to turn to the sounds she had heard in the attic. But she reminded herself firmly that all that had been a weird fucked up stress dream. There hadn't been anything alive in the attic.

The red goop was cool but not cold through the vinyl gloves she was wearing. Georgia scooped up what she could of what was left of the poor animal into one of the black contractor trash bags in the shed, marveling at how handy they had become. Ron had really thought ahead. She salvaged what groceries she could and opted to dispose of the apples before washing the rest of the gore off the walk with a hose. Ralph, still looking confused and distressed, wound himself around her legs, howling. She picked him up in an attempt to comfort him, but he wiggled out of her arms. He padded over to his empty food dish and stuck a paw into it. Banging the little metal against the fresh tile of the kitchen floor.

"Fuck."

Ralph continued rattling his empty bowl. She had forgotten to get him food at the store. Ralph looked at her in a desperate attempt to convince her he was starving. He was as good as an actor as she had been in the VIP room. Almost, he had put on some girth in the short time she had been feeding him, and his growing belly betrayed his ruse.

"Fuck," she repeated.

It had taken her nearly three hours to get to the store outside of town and back. She'd had to pack her cold and frozen items in a cooler on the way home so they wouldn't melt to avoid going into the shit hole of a town that had never grown up. The raccoon had scared her as it was intended. But now she was angry. Fury blazed behind her eyeballs. She was not the fat little defenseless kid she had been. Blackberry Ridge killed that kid years ago and had gifted Georgia with the hard ass exterior that had kept her safe over twenty-five years and at least ten strip clubs in five states. She stared down pimps and made strip club managers cry. To be scared would be to let them win.

She got into her car and drove straight into town before Ralph starved to death.

Mike grinned from behind the counter of the feed store as the bell rang Georgia's arrival. She grinned right back at him, trying to discern if he had been or knew who was behind the dismantling of the raccoon. The entire community consisted of less than two thousand people, there were very few if any secrets here.

"Howdy," he said, still wearing his too wide grin.

"I just need some food for Ralph," she didn't bother with the façade this time. He was not her friend.

"I gottcha. Have to charge you this time though. You decide on staying for a while? Didn't see a for sale sign at the property yet."

"Oh yeah? You didn't see it? You been up that way lately?" Her eyes narrowed. She knew he lived in the house behind the store. He would have no reason to drive by her house.

"Oh, you know how news travels up here. Not much goes unnoticed."

"Yeah, I guess not. This town is pretty weird like that."

She handed him two twenties for the cat food, "Keep the

change, you know for last time." She grabbed the bag and turned to leave.

The bell clanged again as she opened the door to leave.

"You be safe up there, Georgia." The grin never left his face.

Fury ran hot through her blood as she drove back to her house. She dropped the bag of food on the floor and stabbed with a pair of kitchen shears before filling Ralph's bowl.

"Eat up little fucker," she said. He sniffed it and walked away.

She thought about texting Eric to tell him about the dead raccoon. But he might only react badly. Maybe going to look for the culprit, but that wouldn't solve anything. She thought about calling the police, but that was an even worse idea. Eric would be back tomorrow, and they would finish cleaning out the attic. Her stomach clenched as she tried to picture his reaction to the mannequins in the attic, but Georgia knew she was being ridiculous. She'd already laid some heavy shit on him. An attic full of dolls wasn't going to faze him.

Out in the country, cable TV wasn't a thing. The internet was already sketchy as hell, but Georgia needed something to kill the time before Eric came back. She had switched the electricity and the gas in her name, but if she wanted to watch anything on her TV, she would need a satellite service or a DVD player. The latter she hadn't owned in a decade. Only a matter of hours, but it might have been years. She dug through one of her boxes and found a tattered paperback and began to read. An old Clive Barker novel. The snarky demon caught in the pages took her attention until finally she thought she would be able to close her eyes.

A KNOCK at the door woke her up. Not really a knock but a pounding. Her heart began pounding in sympathy. A cop knock. No one else would knock like that. She sat up in bed, terrified. She felt stupid in her assumption that Ann hadn't reported her. How had she ever thought she could get away with something like that? The law tended to frown upon punching innocent realtors in the face. It didn't matter that Ann hadn't been so innocent. If the choice was believing a realtor or a filthy probably drug addicted stripper, Georgia would be on the losing end.

She might be able to argue self-defense. Not that she could prove that. But if they happened to look inside those trash bags, sitting suspiciously by the burn barrel and not by the garbage cans, she was going to spend the rest of her life in prison. But that didn't mean she had to make it easy for them. They could bust down the door and come get her. She pulled the covers over her head. Ralph got up from the foot of her bed and climbed up over her head that was hidden under the blanket. A game for him.

"George!" Eric yelled as he pounded again on the door. Like a cop.

She threw the cover off of her, along with Ralph, and ran to the door. Eric didn't seem at all upset that she was naked. He picked her up and spun her around on the front porch. The warmth of his body mixed with the chill of the morning air. She kissed him long and deeply. The racoon stared at her from the railing. Her mind replaced it with the vision of whoever had left it. Maybe watching them through binoculars. Sick fucks. She kissed him again. Get a good look, weirdos.

He carried her inside without putting her down.

"Love the outfit," he said with a dry smile.

"Oh, do you? I picked it out special." She set her feet down on the cool floor, "So hey, maybe I should get you a key so you're not knocking on my door like the fucking FBI."

"Ooo….a key? That sounds serious."

She kissed him again. She wanted it to be serious. Maybe she needed it to be, but love wasn't her thing. She hadn't chased it. Didn't think she wanted it. But here it was banging on her door like the police. Part of her wanted to blow it all up. Just tell him to fuck all the way off. Maybe punch him in the face. It might even be easier than dealing with the hard-boiled emotion that had invaded her whole core. She was the cat that hadn't expected to catch its prey, and now that she had it, she couldn't figure out just what the fuck to do with it.

"I brought the truck. I loaded it up with the stuff in the front yard," he said finally letting her go.

"You did all that when I was sleeping? Even the…uh…trash bags?"

"Yeah, figured I'd get a jump on it. I got Phil to take over my shifts this week. And Ken owed me a favor. A big one, so he's going to pay me for the missed hours too. I'm all yours until Sunday."

Ken, the owner of Cherry's was a known hard ass. Georgia suspected, no, that was bullshit, Georgia *knew* that he was involved in some shady ass shit. Shit she knew better than to ask about. Which meant that whatever favor he owed Eric, she didn't want to know about either. Once again, though when it came to shady ass shit, Georgia was not in any position to throw any stones.

"Fucking bitchin. Sorr…." She started to say but Eric stifled her words with his mouth.

"Don't you ever apologize to me. Show me the rest of the attic?"

That was about the last thing she wanted to do.

"I'll show you my bed again," she raised an eyebrow. Sort of.

"Later, George. The sooner we deal with this, the sooner it will be over."

She wasn't sure she liked this serious side of him. It felt wrong somehow. She didn't need a hero or a savior. As if he were her big brother instead of her long-time friend and lover. She stood with him in the foyer of her dead father's house naked staring at him. Smothered by his concern, a feeling she had longed for her entire life. A warm blanket that would inevitably become a ball and chain. She opened her mouth to tell him to get the fuck out of her life.

"Fuck," was all that came out.

She didn't bother to shower the sleep and cat hair off of her from the night before and pulled on an old T-shirt and worn leggings. A cold dark lump formed in her belly as she watched him pull down the ladder to the attic. She climbed up behind him and pushed the button to open the secret door before she had too much of a chance to think about it. She waited for his scream.

"Wow," was all he said.

"I know…"

In the daylight, the mannequins were more disturbing than they had been in the shade of dusk, soaking in the fumes of rot and cat shit. They were the Halloween display that the bodies in the closet should have been. Just creepy decorations. She saw them now as Eric must see them. Weird, but harmless. A strange display fueled by a deranged mind. A mind she shared genetics with. Fear overtook her. If this were Eric's dead father's delusion, if she were in his shoes, would she run away screaming? Maybe just back out slowly. This isn't going to work out, it's not you, it's me. Any rational human being would.

Eric and Georgia are part of the same irrational world. A community of misfits, where weird was normal. She didn't have any friends or acquaintances outside of it, as with most of the people she worked with. Polite society wouldn't piss on any one of them if they were on fire. Sure, they might preach about free expression or talk about how they had such admiration for the confidence it took to work in such an industry, but they became perverts and whores once they were out of earshot. Exotic entertainment in the fake smoke and black lights. To be respected. Maybe even admired for their courage to perform the way many outsiders wished they could. Or envied for finding empowerment in their own sexuality and enjoyment in their choosing to be objectified. But they became degenerates again once the bachelor party was over. The Berry Folk had in a way prepared her for a career in the sex industry. In that respect, she supposed they had done her a favor. She couldn't give any fucks about what polite society thought about her now. That went double for the Berry Folk.

Ralph joined them in the attic and began to weave his way in between the black robes that brushed the floor, making them shiver. Eric walked toward one of the figures with its outstretched arms and attempted to give it a handshake. Its shiver turned into a wobble. Then it toppled over, spilling its head out of its robe and onto the floor. The head rolled toward Eric's foot, and he gave it a gentle kick, sending it in Georgia's direction. She wanted to scream, but instead tapped it with her toe, returning it to him.

"Ya know, with all the weird fucked up things we've seen over the years, this ain't shit," he began to laugh. "Like remember the actual shit?"

She did remember the actual shit. Or the story of it. Thankfully she hadn't been a witness, only heard the story second hand. Apparently, someone, presumably a day shift entertainer or possibly a staff member, shit on the floor of the dressing room bathroom. Directly next to the toilet. She began to laugh. The absurdity of this whole situation hit her all at once, obliterating for a moment the horror of it all.

"I do, good times," she laughed along with him as he bunted the mannequin head back to her.

Eric caught his breath, "If we break these down, we can fit them in the truck with everything else. One quick trip to the dump and it's all good."

Georgia nodded at him and moved toward one of the still standing mannequins. In total there were only five. A kind of sadness replaced her laughter. That a man's entire existence could fit in the back of a little pick up was both pathetic and utterly depressing. That this man was her father made it all worse.

Eric picked up the headless body on the floor and unzipped its robe. In seconds it was a pile of parts. Georgia moved on to the next one. Eric got to the last one and stripped it of its clothing as Georgia began to throw the pieces of the others down the ladder and to the floor of the bedroom. They loaded all of it into the back of the truck.

"Alright, you ready?" He said and brushed off his hands on his dirty jeans.

"Sure, let's do this."

The ride to the dump was longer than either of them

expected. Georgia couldn't get her phone to find the location until they were passed the town. But they made it.

As they dumped more garbage on top of garbage, someone said, "Hey, what do you got in those trash bags? A body. Maybe two?"

She looked around and saw no one, but Eric.

Her brain kept telling her it was only a matter of time. Someone would go digging through the trash and find the remains of Ron's victims. Didn't matter that the idea of someone randomly searching garbage at the dump was ludicrous. And even if they did decide there must be some valuable treasure amidst the chicken bones, cheese wrappers, and old diapers, what were the chances they would happen upon this one bag in particular. Georgia's brain told her that not only were those chances fabulous, but also likely that there would be some evidence on the bodies that would lead to her. Not to Ron, but to her. And how long after that, would they drag the pond? Could there be a more obvious place to dump a body and its car? She had to remind herself that was only a dream, not even a nightmare per se, but a dream. As the memory of her fist connecting with Ann's face surfaced, her mind finished the memory with a fantasy. Trying to convince her that Ann's body rested in the pond. Trying to convince her that she was her father's daughter in all respects. That she had inherited her father's legacy. Lunacy.

As they drove away from the dump Georgia looked at Eric and said, "Ok, so I know this is super stupid. Like I am totally aware this is irrational, but I gotta ask..." She paused. He didn't respond. "Do you think there is any chance, like any chance at all that someone might find that bag and open it? Is there any way it could be traced back to me? Us?"

"Not a chance, George. Even if they did, you just found a bag of garbage on the property your estranged father left you. It stunk. Didn't look inside. Plausible deniability."

She could feel him think it. That the rumors about her father and the strange things happening at his property, insolated her. She didn't want to give him a chance to voice that thought because she was sure he was thinking that too. It was what she was thinking. She didn't want to voice it out loud. She didn't believe in jinxes. Still, she didn't want to jinx it.

Could all of this have been avoided if she had only gone to the police? If she had called them and told them then about the corpses in the attic. But she knew how that would play out. As did Eric. They were miscreants. The club may have a cop or two that was sympathetic to them and it's possible that their sympathy extended to a staff member or two, but cops were not their friends. To cops not on the take or that didn't enjoy a favor or two from a desperate entertainer, they were druggies and prostitutes. Even if they weren't. They would be looked at in the worst possible light. No matter that Cherry's was for the most part a clean and upscale club. Not even relatively speaking. They catered to the out-of-town businessman and the fraternity guys. Not that a blue-collar place would be more likely to be involved in sketchy dealings, but Cherry's was a nice place. It was clean, depending on your definition of the word, no fights, or complaints. And, if she were being honest, probably was involved in some sketchy dealings. Even the religious zealots who picketed and protested its opening had decided there were bigger problems to fight. Going to the police, even without Ann's accident, would have landed her in jail. Evidence or not. And while she had sat in many laps of lawyers, she wouldn't be able to defend herself. And now that she was no longer sitting on their boners and whispering in their ears, those lawyers wouldn't be likely to acknowledge that they ever knew her, let alone defend her pro bono. Georgia had done the only thing that made sense to someone in her position. And Eric might be the only person who would really understand that.

The house now cleansed of its madness felt lighter as they

stepped into the sunlit foyer where there lied a sunlit Ralph. There was the shed that would need to be dealt with at some point. But that was just an old truck and some tools. And some lime. There was that too. But that could wait. For now, they had the whole afternoon to just be.

Eric made them sandwiches which although she had a very respectable dining table in her very respectable home, they ate outside on the back porch. The afternoon passed in a very pleasant way. Long conversations about everything and anything, a light dinner and a long walk at dusk.

Later, much later, sometime in the middle of the night, Eric woke her.

"George," he shook her gently, his voice laced with panic. "George. Did you hear that?"

Still groggy, she listened, "No."

"Someone whispering."

She listened again, more awake, "Still nothing. There's a ton of weird noises out here. It's all good. Animals or something." Georgia kissed him in the dark and closed her eyes again.

Then she heard it.

Whispers in the dark. Coming from the attic.

"Animals. It's just animals, or a trick of the wind," she turned to snuggle him. Hopefully back to sleep. "Just squirrels in the attic," she cringed in the dark.

"It sounds like words, George," he said, wrapping his arms around her.

"I know. Just a trick. I heard some weird stuff my first night too. Just raccoons or something. I know the house looks new, but it's old as hell. I promise it's nothing." She was almost certain it was nothing. But not quite. The raccoon stared at her from inside her skull. "Go back to sleep and we'll check it out in the morning."

She waited for a reply and got nothing but the sound of his deepening breath.

13

Georgia awoke alone. Or not alone, but with her feline companion and not her human one. The scent of coffee drifted into her room. She laid there for a moment. Relishing the warm soft sheets on her bare skin as she pictured Eric standing outside, probably naked too, holding a cup of coffee on the porch waiting for her to join him. Working on the assumption that her new, albeit temporary, house was a clothing optional establishment, she padded bare foot and naked to the kitchen and poured herself a cup of coffee then made her way to the back porch.

"Good mo…"

The porch was empty.

He was gone. Because of course he was. What kind of a nut would stay after all this shit? She stared out at the back part of what she was now becoming almost comfortable thinking of as her property and sipped her coffee. She grimaced at the taste. In her hurry to get out to sip it with Eric she hadn't put anything in it. Black coffee was not her jam, but it did wake her up enough to reconsider Eric abandoning her.

Obviously, he was in the bathroom. She didn't remember

noticing the door to either bathroom closed, but that simply meant that she hadn't noticed. Not that he wasn't currently occupying one of them. And while they had known each other for a very long time, and as the bitter shock of the black coffee hit her, it seemed more likely that he had snuck into the bathroom while she was sleeping. He was that kind of guy. Probably had a book of matches or a small bottle of Poo-Pourri with him. Her heart swelled with the thought of such unmanly consideration. But it tracked with the fact that he had yet to leave the seat up. Besides, if he were going to bail, it didn't make any sense to do it *after* becoming criminally complicit. Georgia giggled to herself. One day she may seek therapy for these intrusive thoughts. Or maybe she would just turn them all into a horror novel.

Ralph joined her on the porch, greeting her by forcefully mashing his face into her leg. She sipped more coffee and waited. And waited. Georgia's mind began to drift as the caffeine seeped into her thoughts, shaping and driving them without conscious effort on her part. The best revenge her rogue brain told her was living well, but who cared if the subjects of her revenge couldn't see her. The Berry Folk might revel in their fantasy of her sucking dick behind some urban dumpster in a vain attempt to score her next fix. Which may or may not turn out to be the one that landed her in the county morgue and then to a pauper's grave in some dirt field. Maybe revenge was a dish better served not cold, but hot and in their smug fucking faces. What if she stayed here, rubbing her success (at what she had no idea), and happiness in the wounds of their disappointment. But that was petty bullshit thinking. She had worked far too hard to let go of this place and the fucked-up people that lived here to give any fucks about what they thought of her now or ever. She thought she might rather see the town burn to the ground than live here just to spite them.

Georgia smiled.

Her coffee gone, or almost gone she went back inside. As she set her coffee mug on the counter, she thought she saw a faint footprint at the door to the pantry. Sending a shock of fear down her spine. She bent down to look closer, but it seemed to fade into the pattern of the tile. Just a phantom of footprint, yet another trick her brain tried to pull on her. When her prankster brain tried to remind her of the secret tunnel, she snapped the door on her mind.

The door to the front bathroom was open, in her bedroom she found the bathroom door standing open as well. She couldn't imagine why he would be in there, but she checked the second bedroom which was empty as expected.

The attic.

The little door in the ceiling was closed. If he had gone up there, it seemed weird that he would pull up the ladder, but there wasn't anywhere else he could be in the house. She opened the door and pulled down the ladder. She poked her head and called for him. But was greeted with only silence and an empty room.

With her stomach in her throat, she stepped back down and began to pull on the clothes from the day before, intending to look around the property for him. Unless he really did leave, just decided to do her one last solid and helped her dispose of her father's victims, before taking off for good, he must be outside. She opened her front door, stepped out to the driveway and saw the spot where the borrowed truck had been sitting empty.

Georgia squeezed her eyes shut. Refusing to entertain the idea that she might leak tears from them. Then she heard the crunch of gravel. She opened her eyes and watched as Eric's Honda rolled toward her. She let out the breath she didn't know she had been holding. He turned off the engine and opened the door.

"Hey babe, sorry. I wanted to get the truck back. Didn't want to wake you," he was smiling. She wanted to throw something at him but smiled back instead. He was holding a small brown paper bag.

"What did you bring me?"

He put the bag behind his back as if she hadn't seen it and frowned, "Not really for you, but the house."

Georgia scrunched her nearly paralyzed eyebrows together, "The house?"

"Yeah, come on I'll show you. Promise you won't be mad?" He said as they walked together inside.

"That's a promise I'm not stupid enough to make," she said with way less malice than she intended.

He shrugged and closed the front door. Eric reached into the bag and pulled out a bundle of light grayish green dried leaves tied together with a maroon string.

"Sage," when she just looked at him and cocked her head, he said, "To smudge the house."

"What the actual fuck?" This is why love is bullshit. Most of her life she spent listening to the rumors of occult meetings and ghosts and crazy shit about her dad and weird stuff going on at the house that was now hers. "The house isn't haunted. Ghosts aren't real, and my dad wasn't holding occult meetings or whatever. He was a crazy old man, that's it." Her calm faltered as she spoke, and she spat the last words at him letting malice do all the heavy lifting.

He dropped the sage back into the bag and let it fall to the floor.

"It's just some herbs, George." He tried to put his arms around her, but she stayed rigid, and he ended his awkward embrace. "Look, something was weird last night. I know you heard it too. We don't know the story of what or who was in the attic. But I just wanted to hedge our bets here, ya know?"

"It's stupid. And I am just ready to get out of here and move on. I thought I was done with this place. Please, I need you on my side. And not buying into the bullshit rumors and stories. Obviously, my dad did some shit, or who knows those people could have shown up dead and he just didn't know what to do with them." The raccoon stared at her again from inside her skull. "We know his 'gatherings' were just those old mannequins. Ultimately, I'm not sure I give a fuck. I've been officially put out to pasture by Cherry's...."

He cut her off, "No, babe. You know we can figure that out, we'll go to Ken, and he'll let you back on nights. You're hot as fuck and..."

"Thanks, but we both know that's a load of horseshit. I've done my time. I've run my course. What am I supposed to do? Dance 'til I fall and break a hip? There's nothing sexy about perimenopause... I already had dudes who had yet to grow hair on their balls calling me a MILF or telling me how much they love older women for fuck's sake."

"Peri-what?"

"Never mind. Look this was supposed to be a good thing. A little good luck at the end of a dead-end career. Instead of a retirement party and pension I got a dead dad and a house. And I am hoping I can still make the best of it. Chasing ghosts that don't exist isn't going to help with that."

"Ok. I'm sorry."

She was waiting for him to say she was right but decided that a *sorry* would suffice. She relaxed and gave in to his embrace.

"I'm ready to call another realtor, fuck it, maybe I'll just call one of those Cash for houses outfits. Whatever. I just want to move on and figure the out the rest of my life."

He looked up at the ceiling, then down at her, "I get it. Whatever you want to do, I got you."

"Thank you."

"Wait. Another realtor? Did you lose one?"

"Something like that," like the black robed mannequins in

the attic, she hadn't been really excited to tell him about punching her old bully in the face when she showed up as her realtor. "The realtor the lawyer recommended turned out to be an old classmate. We...uh...weren't getting along."

He looked at his shoes, and she got the impression he was about to say something she didn't want to hear. He opened his mouth and confirmed her thought, "We should probably go through the shed though. House seems good to go, but probably not the worst thing to take a look-see and at least clean it out."

Georgia rolled her eyes. Not just at Eric but the whole damned thing. The cascade of bizarre events seemed to never end. She hadn't bothered to explore the shed, other than for the things she needed. He was right of course. The house and attic were good to go, and the rest of the property looked cool too, if there were any more hidden bullshit, it would be in the shed.

"That sounds awful. But yeah, you're right." As much as she wanted to be rid of the house, she was reluctant to make any other move. She had a nasty habit of taking things from bad to worse. She wanted an escape, a break from the madness and reprieve from everything. And she still had to consider the monumental issue of what the hell she was going to do with the rest of her life. Eric plucked the paper bag holding the bundle of sage and walked it to the kitchen garbage and dropped it in. "Hey, how about we go see a movie and have dinner in the city? I want to get the fuck out of the country for a little while."

"Perfect," Eric said and pulled her close.

Georgia couldn't see the look of terror on Eric's face as she sped through the turns on the way out of Blackberry Ridge. She was laser focused on the road in front of her. If she had, she wouldn't have slowed. They spent the afternoon and evening eating and entertaining themselves. There was no talk of bodies, or realtors, or ghosts.

Night had fallen as they drove the dark hills back to the house in the hills. The sunroof revealed a sky littered with stars and she thought Eric might strain his neck staring up at it. As they pulled down into her driveway, she turned to him and said, "We could get a blanket and fuck under those stars."

"Look at you with all the great ideas," he leaned in to kiss her as she put the car in park.

They pulled away from each other, but as she reached for her door release, she saw a figure, its white clothing glowing in the moonlight, dart behind the small shed.

"George," Eric whispered. "Did you see that?"

She just nodded.

"Stay here," he said and pulled on his door handle.

The door swung open on silent hinges. Eric stepped out. His soft soled dress shoes made no noise as he took large strides toward the garage. She opened her door and put a foot on the gravel. He looked back, frowned at her, and motioned for her to stay back. She just shrugged. He was a fool if he thought she was going to sit in the car.

Eric reached under his sport coat and pulled a small knife from his belt. Holding it near his thigh. Georgia treaded carefully behind him, highly aware that one misstep in her high heels would either make enough noise to alert whoever was hiding behind the shed or cause her to break an ankle. Or hip.

He slipped behind the small building, and in seconds came out on the other side. Still searching for the trespasser. Georgia met him at the door, he had his hand on the handles of the double doors. Although, she couldn't see how anyone could have gotten inside without them seeing. He looked at her before turning it and pulling it open. She followed behind him. Seeing the same cluttered but devoid of humans, space as he did. Confident there was no one hiding inside, they went outside. Carefully searching the perimeter for any sign of the person they saw.

Eric put his head through the entrance to the attic and scanned it with a flashlight. Together they searched the inside of the locked house and again found nothing. No sign of anyone other than Ralph who gave no indication he had seen anyone. Either alive or dead. Georgia looked at him and broke the silence.

"It wasn't a fucking ghost."

14

It didn't matter that he never tried to tell her the figure that seemed to disappear behind the shed was a ghost. She could feel the thought oozing from him. He had brought the sage bundle because he assumed the house was haunted. She looked it up. That's what sage was used for. To clear a space of bad spirits. She wouldn't have been surprised if he picked it up in one of the shops on the main street of Blackberry Ridge. Which really pissed her off. The tension manifested into its own haunting entity. One that hovered over them for the next two days. It would fade and they would talk like normal, but then a slight movement of air from an open window would become a cold draft, raise the hairs on the back of their necks, and their own personal phantom would fade back in to fuck up their groove. When the day came that he to go back to work, she was relieved. But she still felt the need to exercise the ghost that had materialized between them. If it pissed him off and he left for good? So, fucking what? She'd come this far without a guy.

"Hey, before you take off, let's go check out the shed," she said, but what she meant was, *Let's go see how someone dressed as a ghost could have made it look like they disappeared.* While she didn't know the answer, she did know that the "gatherings" were just life-sized dolls, and her father was clever enough to make that hidden door. Not to mention the nifty cat tunnel. She had no doubt that someone intended to scare them, as she had no doubt that there was a rational explanation for how they did it so convincingly. Even the "whispering" in the attic could be faked. The disemboweled raccoon was only the first thing, this fucking ghost thing was the second. Games played by assholes.

"Sure."

They walked down the small path from the driveway to the rough wooden shed. She kept her eyes on the ground, looking for anything that might help her convince her…boyfriend?… that the being they saw was a person. Georgia was about to tell him about the raccoon, and how someone from town was just fucking with her and realized that she was being incredibly stupid. She needed him to believe it was a ghost. At least for now. For the exact same reason, she hadn't told him about the raccoon. If he knew that someone was sneaking onto the property, he not only wouldn't leave, but he might seek to find that person. That could get bad. Really bad. She wasn't scared of the Berry Folk. She didn't think any of them had the nerve to do anything other than stupid pranks. Georgia had so far still been able to convince herself that a mutilated animal was just a prank. She didn't need this more complicated than it already was. And Eric going into savior mode would only make things worse.

A thing about communities, particularly one as stigmatized as the one that she and Eric shared, was that they were extremely protective of one another. Even strippers, women with latent insecurities thrown together and made to compete with each other for the same dollar bills based on their looks, banded together when the situation called for it. That went double for the male staff. There was the occasional whiff of toxic masculinity, and maybe a glimmer of misogyny, but they were the outlier and not the norm. Bouncers, managers… Jake being the exception at Cherry's, and DJs not only had a vested financial interest in keeping the entertainers safe and happy, but they also had a human one too. Dealing with a drunk bachelor party or a gaggle of hammered airmen wasn't easy. Throw in the arrogant self-absorbed attorney or self-proclaimed entrepreneur who felt like their status entitled them to treat women like shit, and anyone with even a slight sense of empathy would feel the need to protect them. Georgia had almost been surprised when Eric only had a knife on him and not a gun. While she had never physically seen a firearm at the club, she knew that there was always a staff member who was packing.

She could convince him that ghosts were bullshit another time. But for now, she didn't need him to know about whoever was sneaking onto her property. She wasn't afraid. And she had her own fucking gun. Having him here was awesome, but she hadn't grown comfortable with the idea of a relationship. If she thought about it too deeply, the very idea of having a boyfriend would start to feel like wearing concrete shoes.

The door to the old building creaked when it was opened, and while she wasn't looking to point out how the ghost person had disappeared anymore, she was paying attention. They would have likely heard the door open if they had left through the shed. The wooden door that sat on unoiled hinges was made of thin plywood as the rest of the shed. The weather hadn't done it any favors, and as they entered it, she wondered if the thing would still be standing after the next winter storm. She pulled the string that turned on the paltry light.

"Maybe we should just light a match," she said.

"It looks like the only thing holding it up is stuff inside," Eric said. The small pickup truck and the workbench which looked to be half rotted filled, almost the entire space. Eric groped some of the tools on the work bench. Picking each one up, turning them over with admiration. "These are new. Or close to it. And he's got a ton of them. For real, I wouldn't be surprised if he did all that work inside himself."

"Right on. I don't care. How do we get rid of all this stuff," she almost corrected herself to say 'I', but let it slide. This was ultimately her house, her problem, he had been a huge help, but her anti-social tendencies were kicking in again. She just wanted him to leave. She hadn't yet decided for good or not. But she had befriended most of the demons in her head, and she had been neglecting them lately. Missing them even.

"It would be a shame to trash all these tools," he spoke about them as if they were precious jewels. "We could sell them; eBay maybe?"

Georgia hoped she was only cringing on the inside, "I don't want to bother with all that. Do you want them?"

His eyes widened, "Sure, but George, wouldn't the money help?"

It would, but her focus was on getting out of here. Starting with him. She wanted some time alone with her racing anxious thoughts. If she let them all duke it out, eventually they would put themselves in some kind of order and she could figure out how to get out of this town and move on. With or without a man. Also, she didn't want him around when she went digging through the last bit of Ron's things.

"Yes, but I'll figure it out. I tell you what, why don't you take what stuff you think is good here and try to unload it for me. I'll clean out the rest of the stuff here, and when you get back, we'll run it to the dump. Most of it looks like garbage anyway," she grabbed him and pulled him close. Or closer, as the space was tight already. "Or there's always a can of gas and a match."

"Yeah, that's what I'm afraid of. Are you sure you're ok here by yourself?"

She punched him. But not in the face. And not that hard.

"I ain't 'fraid of no ghosts…."

"Ooo…quoting 80s movies now. Don't date yourself old lady."

She punched him hard this time, but still not in the face. He rubbed his shoulder where she had hit him and frowned at her. He filled up a nearby tool bag with the bulk of the tools and took them to his car. She gave him one last kiss, hoping he couldn't sense her wanting him to leave, and she watched him drive up and away. Her shoulders relaxed and her mind cleared. As if he had taken the weight of her thoughts along with him.

Georgia almost skipped up the short walk to her front door, where just inside, Ralph laid in the sun. He opened one eye to acknowledge her existence.

"I take back what I said about wanting to hang out with someone who doesn't shit in a box," she said, as she stepped over him.

She filled a bottle with ice water and picked up her portable speaker and phone and skipped back out to the shed. The mid-morning sunshine warmed the fallen leaves she crushed under her sneakers. She propped open the shed doors, so that she didn't have to rely on the filthy old light bulb. She set her phone on the workbench, and it began to spit out metal riffs from the small speaker.

She turned it up. "This one goes to eleven," she giggled, suddenly aware that there wasn't anyone to get her old movie reference.

But then again maybe there was.

People didn't scare her. Not in a physical way. While she had to admit that some if not most of, fuck it, maybe all of her bravado came from the fact that she had always had a couple hundred pounds of bouncer hovering over her. She was five feet and five inches of 'fuck around and find out,' at least in her own head. Whoever was fucking with her wasn't going to hurt her. Of that, she was pretty sure. If anything, they might be trying to scare her off, which was really stupid, because all she wanted to do since she got here was leave. Forever.

There was about a quarter acre of weeds and crab grass between the barbed wire fence that marked the end of her property and the shed. Beyond that, her neighbor's yard began. She doubted that the old lady who had lived there when she was a kid still did. Margaret Baker would have been around a hundred years old by now. Her side of the fence, or whoever's side of the fence was overgrown with thick briar bushes. Even well kept, she wouldn't have been able to see the house beyond. Assuming that it still stood. If she remembered correctly, it was a double-wide prefabricated home. Georgia didn't care all that much if it was occupied or not, but it seemed a likely exit route if someone wanted to come on to her property without using the driveway.

She walked toward the fence, breathing deeply and telling herself she was stupid for wishing the Smith & Wesson 22 caliber revolver a customer had gifted her wasn't still sitting in her nightstand next to her dildo. A duo that had so far pretty much negated her need for a man. But the canopy of oak leaves all but obliterated the sun and its warmth, and she felt the creeps begin to settle in the pit of her stomach. She almost preferred the maggots. She shivered as she neared the tetanus laden barbed wire fence. But even in the falsely darkened light, she could see the answer to the ghost mystery.

Nature's cruel country joke was to facilitate the growth of poison oak next to bushes that in the late springtime would be bursting with plump dark berries. The locals mostly knew better, but she hadn't passed a spring where some kid hadn't come to school sporting an ugly red and purple rash along with juice stained and thorn pricked fingers. Learning to recognize the nefarious leaves was a lesson instilled in her from the time she could walk. Leaves of three, let them be. And she always did, although she would find out later that not everyone who touched the vile plant would get the red raised itchy rash. Mostly only people who are allergic, and even they might be spared when the plant was dormant. Like in fall and winter. Or now. Just beyond the wire, and into the next yard, she saw a person sized hole in the thicket of poison oak. With the shed blocking the view of the fence from the driveway, it would be hard to spot someone ducking in or out of this hole. Bushes, trees, and more poison oak swallowed the fence all the way from the front of the property on this side to the back. A natural security system, but one with just this weak spot.

Other than the tools, the shed seemed to hold most of Don's personal things. She wished the cleaners hadn't ignored the dilapidated building, but they had only been contracted for the house. The tools were new, nothing else was. The bulk looked to be old manuals, paperwork and odds and ends. A few moldering cardboard boxes and plastic bins lived under the workbench and appeared to be protected by an army of unseen spiders. The dirty webs gave away their residence.

Her music still blaring, she opened the door to the tiny pick-up truck. A Datsun. Her head brushed the driver's side visor. Something hard and sharp bit her on the forehead. She jumped, smacking her head on the roof and making it ring. The keys to the truck landed on the seat scaring the dust. She rubbed her head some more and rolled her eyes. She jammed the key into the ignition, expecting exactly nothing. And got nothing. The battery would be as dead as her father by now. She ducked back out of the cab and inspected the tires, which turned out to be only kind of flat, but not all the way. Just enough maybe to roll the thing out of there. She turned the key again, but this time didn't attempt to turn over the engine. She stepped on the brake and shifted the truck into neutral.

"Fucking sweet," she said.

She opened the other door of the shed and went back to the truck, placing her hands on the hood, making grooves in the thick dust. She began to push using her legs, being careful not to aggravate her back, or her knees, until she had the momentum needed to get it to start to roll. Steering wasn't necessary as she only needed it go straight back and out of the shed. Once that was accomplished, she set it back in park, tossed the keys on the seat and brushed her hands on her jeans. She happened to look in the bed as she prepared to walk back into the shed and saw a rusty metal half-moon contraption attached to a chain. She peered over the side and immediately identified the item. A fucking bear trap.

The thing was much heavier than it looked, a firework exploded in the middle of her spine as she fished it out of the truck bed. She ignored it and continued hauling the thing up and out. Her back screamed at her as she looked at it and determined that, while it wasn't in great shape, it was still functional. The color of the rust just so happened to be one of the colors of the fallen leaves that sat on her property line.

"Ha! Fuck you, ghost."

She set the trap at the hole, sprinkling dirt and leaves over the top of it. Brushing her hands off again, she walked back to the shed. With both doors open and without the truck inside, the sunlight pouring into the shed was almost cheery. Not almost, it was cheery. A voice screamed dark lyrics from her speaker and Georgia smiled again.

"Alright, old man. What else you got for me?" She frowned, "Just kidding. I don't want to know."

15

GEORGIA STOOD JUST outside the shed trying to figure out just where to start. It was about twelve maybe fifteen-feet wide and around twice as deep. With the Datsun gone, the task of emptying it out didn't seem daunting, but it also didn't do much for her inclination to just set the thing on fire. She had removed the bear trap from the bed of the truck, but it still held a small gas can. Georgia picked it up and began to sprinkle the contents of it around the inside perimeter of the shed. She reached into her pocket and pulled out a joint and a lighter. She flicked the lighter and touched the flame to the end of the joint, inhaling deeply. She then flicked it again and put the flame to one of the rotting cardboard boxes that now stank of gasoline. It erupted, and in seconds the shed was engulfed. She watched it burn, along with any gruesome surprises that might be inside.

She opened her eyes and flipped the unlit joint and lighter over in her pocket.

She was back where she started, or where she hadn't started. The vision or more accurately...hallucination cleared. The back of the shed held plastic bins which seemed to be in better shape than the cardboard if only because the clear cracked plastic was slightly more intact. It looked as if it held mostly clothing and other soft materials, the stuff under the work bench looked as if it might fall apart if she tried to move it. As she stared at it, she thought she could see it vibrating with the punishing tunes coming out of her portable little speaker. She slid her phone back in her pocket and fondled the lighter again.

"Fuck it."

She pulled out the contents of her pockets and lit the joint, inhaling deeply this time for real. Reluctantly she slipped the lighter back in her pocket. Hoping the weed would cloud her mind enough to just get in there and get it done. Finally deciding that she didn't need to actually go through any of this stuff. It looked to be garbage and that was exactly how she would treat it. She wasn't expecting to find any priceless heirlooms or hordes of cash. She wouldn't be surprised however if she found a dried-up spleen or two. She paused at the thought, there was the fact that the house had been remodeled, and that couldn't have been cheap. But that might also simply be a reason that there wouldn't be any cash left. Besides, she could make her own money, her sanity might be worth risking throwing all this stuff away without checking for any DB Cooper era missing bills. She'd just pull everything out and if the fucking shed was still standing, she'd count herself lucky. With the joint in her hand, she walked into the shed toward the back where the plastic bins looked as if the held up the wall.

An oil-stained piece of plywood sat right in the middle of the hard packed dirt floor, as she stared at the greasy wood, she thought the truck was probably just more garbage. Making a plan to simply load the back of the truck with all the trash from the shed. Perhaps she could have the whole thing just towed away. She stepped on the plywood. The first part was hard, but when she stepped on the oil darkened spot in the middle her shoe plunged through the rotted wood. Now up to her shin, Georgia pointed her foot downward and when it didn't touch the bottom of the hole, she yanked it out. She realized that the piece of plywood served two purposes. One to catch the oil from the leaking old pickup. And the other to hide the hole underneath. Her smoking joint lay nearby, a thin trail of smoke wound its way up to the ceiling.

"Should have lit the fucking thing on fire."

She sat down and looked into the hole, hoping it was just a huge gopher hole. Shit, she'd be happy if it turned out to be a den full of rattlesnakes. Intuition, or maybe just the fact that nothing had as of yet gone as she planned told her that it held stuff that she didn't want to know about but was about to find out anyway. But for the moment all she could see was darkness. But she really didn't need to remove the plywood. There was no good reason that she could think of to actually investigate. That whole plausible deniability thing. What she didn't know, couldn't cause her trouble. Or get her arrested according to Eric. And there was the whole bright side thing. She didn't twist her ankle or strain her knee, or her back for that matter, when she fell. She even made it out without a splinter. And she still owned this weird house in this fucked up town. The oil-stained piece of plywood she was sitting on was ultimately the contingency for her retirement that she had never gotten around to planning for. Taken from that perspective, she was the luckiest ex-stripper she knew of.

The joint had gone out, but the scent of the sweet smoke still lingered in the small dusty space. Its mellowness tempered by the violence that was still blaring from her speaker. The air was cool, but Georgia felt a heat rise up from her chest and spread through her body. Sweat popped out on her upper lip, then up to her forehead and down to her chest. She fanned herself. Adrenaline was her first thought, but hot flash was her second. She leaned over and recovered her joint. Sitting cross-legged, she lit it again and rolled her eyes at her own foolishness. She buried her thoughts in smoke, dropped the roach into the hole, and stood up.

She had always found heavy metal cathartic. In spite of her small stature, in her head she was six foot tall, bulletproof, with a voice like Corey Taylor of Slipknot. Maggot. The aggressive nature of her preferred genre of music fed that perception of herself. It gave her power, but as her eyelids drooped and her hormones set her skin on fire, maybe she needed a different sort of power. A new perspective, she had entered an era of change. Resilience. Positivity even. A tangle of moving threads in her mind grew more complicated as she tried to hold on to the past. She didn't need an Instagram meme or YouTube guru to tell her that change was inevitable, it was the only real guarantee in life besides death. She'd spent her life up until now fighting a losing battle with things she couldn't control. But she had long ago lost sight of what she was fighting for.

Maybe it was the weed, no it was definitely the weed, but Georgia turned off the screaming voice on her phone. The noise coming out of it, suddenly less soothing. She scrolled through her music app, not knowing but also knowing what she would choose. Something chill. A small change, but one that might stimulate a shift in perception. Reggae. She closed her eyes, which welcomed the reprieve from the sunlight, and swayed for a moment to the music. The sweat cooled on her brow as her body relaxed. Her smoke-filled thoughts slowed. She listened with curiosity, exploring, riding the melody into oblivion.

She opened her eyes, and the old workbench swam into view. On it lay the new pair of work gloves she had picked up at the large store beyond Blackberry Ridge. The ones she had found when she was dismantling the Halloween decorations, had gone to the dump with them. She put them on and reached for the first box under the bench. The rubber grip on the gloves helped her pull the thing out from what appeared to have been its home for a long time. It was heavier than she might have thought, but she wasn't tempted to look inside. She simply didn't care. What was in any of these boxes had no bearing on the task at hand. She carried it to the bed of the truck and set it down carefully so as to not accidentally break it open and shatter her hard-fought peace.

She moved on to the next one, and then the next. The spiders had either gone into hiding at the movement or fucked off entirely and deserted their webs long ago. Soon she reached the last box under the bench. She dragged it out, ignoring the top of it, which was tilted slightly open, trying to expose her to its potentially lewd contents. Severed fingers? Maybe a nipple or two? Its open flap teased her, dared her. She picked it up without taking the bait and set it down in the bed of the pickup.

Without the boxes, the bench didn't look as rotten as it had before. In fact, once the back wall was cleared of the plastic bins, she thought it may end up looking like any retiree's little workshop. She could see an old guy making little bird houses to sell at the farmer's market. Glasses perched on his nose, cup of not too strong Earl Grey cooling nearby. Not even a whiff of weird or rotting bodies. Her buzz was wearing off, but her newfound chill seemed to linger.

Careful to avoid the dark hole that may or may not hold human remains, Georgia moved to the back of the shed. Behind the murky plastic of the top bin floated bright colors, that looked suspiciously like a trove of Christmas sweaters, or leftovers from the wardrobe on the Cosby show set. She wasn't going to open the lid to find out of course. The normality of it, the utter totally cool and not weird old man-ness of it was unnerving. Somewhere buried in all that brightly colored faux wool and cotton was the kidney of an unfortunate hitchhiker.

Her father had been distant. He was odd for sure. Eccentric, if she were being nice. But she had never known him to be mean. The only time he had ever yelled that she could remember was the last phone call. It was why she had hung up.

Although, she if were being fair, they had been talking about her mother and sister. The conversation had gone from heavy to heated. And then rocketed past infuriating. He wouldn't stop about the accident. The new stop sign, a cover up. His descent from religion to conspiracies had been a short one. He had gone from odd to crazy. Had he been a father to her, she may have tried to soothe him. To care for him. But he hadn't been that. He had been nothing at all. He was cold, rigid, and distant. But he had never been cruel.

Georgia would have never, ever thought him a murderer. She discovered long ago that she didn't hate the guy. Didn't really dislike him either. Kind of how she didn't dislike Indian food, but only because she had never tried it. That *was* on her bucket list though. She just hadn't made it that far yet. She never knew to love or hate the guy. She had been disappointed, but never afraid of him. He was weird, made himself a target of the town, and her a target by proxy. For that, the relentless taunting and teasing she had endured, she laid directly at his feet. But even that hadn't been malicious. She blamed him, but never thought he had set her up for that intentionally. For all the complicated dynamics of her childhood, the death of the only people that seemed to give a shit about her, she would have never pinned Ron as a killer.

But here she was. Holding a thin plastic bin full of horrible but harmless sweaters, terrified that they concealed evidence of depravity. She could disassociate, pretend they were Halloween decorations, but she ultimately couldn't deny the reality that she had found not one, but two rotting bodies in the attic closet of her dead father's house. And the weirdest thing about all of it, was she couldn't connect the act with the man that had lived here. It simply seemed inconsistent with what she did know of him. As little as that was.

Georgia made it through the rest of the bins, each much like the first. Cloudy almost opaque, the contents weren't completely obvious. But they all seemed innocuous. Rags in one, jeans in another, maybe. Files and paperwork in yet another. She built a protective cocoon around her intentional apathy and snuggled down inside, as she carried each bin to the back of the little pick up. She didn't need to know the contents, because they didn't matter.

Soon, there was nothing left but the bag of lime. And the piece of plywood. She gripped the top of the sack and started to drag it. It was far heavier than anything she had tried to move so far, but she managed to get it next to the truck. She tugged on the top, intending to pick it up and swing it into the back of the truck, but her back protested as she tried to lift it off the ground. She thought better of it and just left it next to the tire. Eric would be back, and he could help.

She stood looking at the now emptied shed. One that if it had held any more secrets, she had successfully avoided uncovering them. The music from the speaker stopped abruptly when it died. She peeled off her gloves and set them on the bench to look at her phone. It was dead along with the speaker. Simultaneous death. She slipped it into her pocket. She looked at her work one more time as she moved to close the door. Other than the work bench, the only thing left was the sheet of oil-stained plywood and its gaping hole. It taunted her as the flap of the box had. Daring her to flip it up and look inside the hole it was concealing. She stared at it. Wishing she had another joint. But she would need to either drive into town to the dispensary, or well outside it to the next town if she wanted any more weed. Neither option was very appealing at the moment.

There was a roach at the bottom of that hole though. She wondered if it wasn't quite the little nub she thought it was. Maybe even enough of it left to get her reasonably high until Eric came back. She hadn't felt like there was anything in the hole when her foot was in it. It could very well simply be an old gopher hole that Ron hadn't wanted to bother to fill in. The dire warnings from when she was a kid of broken ankles caused by unnoticed gopher holes flashed in her mind. And if he needed something to catch the oil of that old clunker, putting down the wood made total sense. Two bodies…. Birds, one stone. She refused to entertain the voice that told her the hole was far too big to be from a gopher. Rodents of unusual size?

Georgia bent down and grasped the edge of the plywood and tugged upward. She closed her eyes as she flipped it up, not seeing the contents of the hole. She changed her mind and dropped it. When the rush of dirty air and dust blew her hair back as it landed back in place, she cautiously opened her eyes.

The hole most certainly contained only dirt….and her roach. She was sure of it. Which she was now convinced was much too small to smoke anyway. It wasn't completely extinguished when she dropped it in. It probably smoked itself to death.

"Well fuck me."

She was totally out of pot.

Ralph was waiting for her as she opened the door. She reached down to scratch the top of his head, and he rose to meet her hand. She smiled at his affection, until he pulled away and led her to his empty food dish. She filled it and gave him fresh water before plugging her phone in to charge on her nightstand. She stripped and got in the shower to rinse away the filth from the old shed.

She was happy. Georgia didn't realize how much she had been anticipating finding something awful. But the scariest thing she had found other than the hideous sweaters, was that her discarded roach was far too small to light up again. Although she hadn't actually found that, just assumed it. It had smoked itself for a while after she dropped it. So, an educated guess. Sure, the bins and boxes could have been hiding something, but if they were, she would never find out. When Eric came back, he could help her figure out how to get rid of the last remaining belongings of Ron, and she could be done with this place and the town for good. For real this time.

She toweled off and checked her phone. She smiled when

she saw the text notification, but it faltered a little when she saw it was Pete and not Eric. She opened the text.

Hey you. Missing you. Where are you at? I would love to see you. I checked the Pink Poodle, but they said you didn't work there.

Georgia took a deep breath and plotted a course of action. Patting herself on the back for her restraint in not telling him to fuck off before. Angel had been fired, and he hadn't found a replacement. Her cash was running low, and self-employed strippers didn't collect unemployment payments. Her relationship with Pete was strictly transactional. But other than receiving the occasional cash *help out* through a pay app, she had always made her money at the club. When she told him she wasn't going back to Cherry's he assumed she had just gone to the other club in town. As if. She wouldn't work at that dump.

Hey! OMG! Miss you too. (kissy face) *I didn't go to the Pink Poodle.*

No. She deleted that sentence and typed instead.

The Pink Poodle wouldn't hire me. I'm not working right now. Not sure what I am going to do. (sad face)

Pete responded immediately. *What?!! That's ridiculous. Oh no.*

Yeah, the door girl never liked me. I can't remember if I told you about my dad's house. She really couldn't remember if she had told him she had inherited it or not.

I remember you telling me. Is that where you are staying?

It is. Still looking for a buyer. Now she remembered telling him the last time she saw him. Before he tried to blow her off for Angel, she had been hoping he might buy the fucking thing. She dared to think that could still be a thing.

Maybe I can come up and take a look? I have been thinking of buying a new rental.

Georgia cringed. She wanted him to give her cash and definitely wanted him to buy this fucking house, but she most certainly didn't want to be alone with the guy in the woods. She could end up rotting in the attic. That was probably a bit paranoid, Pete was almost certainly harmless. Paranoia born out of more stripper baggage. But strict boundaries were the key to not starring in some cat lady's favorite crime show.

How about we meet for dinner instead? She responded.

The pause was much longer than she would have liked. She didn't want him thinking about it. She knew dinner wasn't what he was after. She had never slept with the guy, but not for his lack of trying. She had also never quite turned him down. The possibility, however slight, was part of the fantasy. Her excuse was always that she could get in trouble for meeting him outside of the club. Which was only sort of true. She wouldn't get in trouble per se, but it was frowned upon. The club liked a strict line between call girl and stripper. It kept the club out of the eye of the vice cops trying to sniff out the prostitutes. Or catch them anyway. The vice cops pretty much assumed the girls at the club were all hookers. There were a few of course, but they were the exception. That Pete was hitting her up confirmed that Angel wasn't one of them, or he wouldn't have texted her.

That sounds great! Tonight?

Georgia cringed. It's not that she didn't like Pete. He wasn't awful, but she was still riding her 'I didn't find any corpses in the shed' high. The thought of batting her fake eyelashes at him across a candle lit table while he made awkward innuendos wasn't on her list of things she wanted to do this evening.

Pete must have started to worry about the time she was taking to reply and followed up with another text. *$500 ok?*

Georgia didn't pause this time. *Perfect. Where and when?*

Gino's 7pm?

She liked Gino's, but for $500 she'd have eaten at Burger King. A salad though.

See you then! (four kissy faces she thought about it, then added a fifth)

He sent her a kissy face back and she stuck her tongue out at her phone.

It was five in the afternoon. It would take an hour to get to Gino's, and about forty-five minutes to put her stripper face on and do her hair. That would give her just enough time to stop at the pot shop on her way out of town.

As soon as she put down her phone, it dinged again. This time it was Eric.

Hey honey. Miss you. His text read.

Miss you too. She wrote back, and she mostly meant it this time. She had things under control and liked the fact that she hadn't needed him to get them that way. But she did kind of miss him. *I got the shed all cleaned out. How's the club?*

It blows. So same. I can come back out there tomorrow if you want.

She thought about it. And she did want. She wouldn't mention meeting Pete. Eric didn't need to know that. He might go all 'knight in shining armor' and try and tell her it was dangerous to meet a customer, even if she knew him blah blah blah. Whatever. It was a public place, and the money would come in handy. Plus, if she could get him to bite on the house, it would save her a major headache. Things were finally coming up in her favor.

I do want. (love emoji)

Great. I'm working the night shift, so I will want to sleep in. See you around 1?

Perfect. (more love emojis)

Setting her phone down she got ready to meet Pete. She heard a strange noise, and realized she was humming.

It was full dark when she pulled into the dispensary located right on the edge of Blackberry Ridge. She wondered again just how the fuck they had gotten the town to let them set up shop. She showed her ID to the dreadlocked stoner chick at the door. Her name tag read Dazy, and Georgia tried not to giggle. She must have known something like four or five 'Dazy's' in her time. At least three Roxy's, two Sativa's, and one Lexus. Why you might need a fake name to work at a pot shop, Georgia didn't know. But this chick's name sure as shit, wasn't Dazy. She also wondered if this Dazy wasn't from Blackberry Ridge. She thought she might like this Dazy.

"What do you got...Dazy?"

Dazy looked at her and smiled, "I remember you from last time. Are you enjoying being back in town?"

Maybe perimenopausal brain fog or simply smoking too much pot, but Georgia didn't remember having a conversation with Dazy when she had been here the first time.

"Um, sure. Memory lane. Amiright?" Georgia was starting to doubt her original assessment about Dazy. Maybe she *was* Berry Folk.

"I wouldn't have wanted to grow up here," she said. "These people are kind of weird."

Georgia couldn't read her. Was she baiting her into talking shit? Was she being genuine? Georgia studied her face. Dazy didn't look like the type that would decapitate a raccoon or impersonate a fantom. But her stripper sense told her to proceed with caution.

"Small towns are…. different. I only have a few minutes and am totally dry. Does the chef have any specials this evening?"

Dazy locked eyes with her in an expression Georgia still failed to read, "In fact he does." She flashed a smile full of teeth. "Purple monster pineapple cush, is my favorite and it's on sale. Comes with two pre rolls and because you seem cool, I'll throw in a four pack of gummies."

"Sold!" Georgia flashed her own teeth. She wasn't into edibles after once misreading dosing instructions and spending a day in bed mostly nauseous. But all of a sudden, she was in a hurry to bat her eyelashes at Pete over a plate of overpriced and undercooked pasta. She reached into the pocket of her skintight jeans and pulled out her cash. When the transaction was complete, she dropped the change in the tip jar on the counter. Dazy smiled at her.

As Georgia grabbed her brown paper bag of weed, Dazy said, "You be careful up there, I hear it's haunted."

Georgia didn't bother to try to read her face this time, as she reached into the tip jar and removed the money, she had just deposited.

"Fuck you," she said as the bells jingled on door as she left.

She was fuming as she sped through the hills on the way to meet her old customer. Georgia swore no matter what, she wasn't going to go back into town for anything. And fuck it. She was going to get Pete to buy the fucking house tonight. Even if it cost her a blow job. Well maybe not that. But things had gotten really weird, and it couldn't hurt to stay flexible. Georgia didn't discount that fact that she might really be paranoid, but she also couldn't shake the impression that the whole town might be in on the harassment. Trying to drive her crazy. Trying to drive her out of a house and a town she didn't want to be in. Or it could simply be a town with a disproportionate amount of assholes. Logic and reason told her it was the latter.

Had they done this to her father? Driven him crazy? Driven him to murder? Her illogical brain told her.

She jammed her finger upward into the button that caused the moon roof to slide open as another hot flash hit her. The cool air evaporating her sweat before it could dampen her light blue low-cut sweater. Pete had to be her focus now. The guy was loaded, at least she was pretty sure he was. And desperately wanted to fuck her. Anybody probably. But right now, it was her. And she needed to get out of this bullshit.

Gino's Italian bistro sat under the yellow glow of a string of globes lights. The parking lot was full, and she had to park across the street. Pete was waiting for her at the entrance holding a bouquet of roses. She buried her face in the petals as she took them into her hands, delaying the tight hug that would come when she looked up. She plastered a smile on her face as Pete wrapped her in his arms.

There was an hour wait for a table, but a palmed hundred-dollar bill in Pete's hand to the hostess got them seated immediately. It was by the bathroom, but Georgia didn't care. She was hungry despite her fury and latent anxiety, and she didn't want to spend an hour not only starving but making small talk while Pete stared at her tits.

"How have you been?" Pete's enthusiastic tone was alarming, but Georgia matched it anyway.

"Omg! Things have been kind of weird." She smiled at her gross understatement. Pete took it as a good sign. "So, the house is awesome. Totally remodeled. A cute little shed in the yard, finished attic room. It's really great."

"But you don't want to stay?" She didn't like that tone at all. Not quite suspicious, but she would need a really good story to cover the real one.

Most of her conversations with customers, especially long-term regulars, were a blend of fiction and reality. Revealing too much truth could be dangerous if one of them happened to morph into a stalker, but they wanted to know the 'real' her, which demanded a certain amount of authenticity. Sometimes she had a hard time remembering just what she had told who. Slipping up and saying the wrong thing might betray the ruse. Georgia was now trying to parse out just how much truth she had told Pete about her family and Blackberry Ridge. She was walking a tight rope where if she fell, she would have to try and sell the property through traditional channels. Whereas, if she maintained her balance, she could put the whole mess behind her.

"You know, small towns aren't really for me," she looked at him over the rim of her glass of Pinot Noir.

"I remember you telling me that Blackberry Valley was tough place to grow up."

She let out a breath. He knew about the bullying. Perfect.

"Ridge."

"Huh?"

"It's Blackberry Ridge, not Valley. But who cares. Yeah, not a lot of great memories there. I'm grateful for the house, but ready to move on."

Pete's eyes brightened. Georgia cringed on the inside. He took 'move on' for 'marry Pete'. Not good, and why she had never met a customer outside of the club.

"I can see why. I don't…"

The food arrived at the table cutting him off.

"It really is a great house though," she said, hoping the wine and her utter desperation wasn't causing her to oversell it.

"I'd love to see it," he said. He slurped a noodle, leaving sauce at the corners of his mouth.

"I have pictures," Georgia pulled out her phone and began to show him.

"Wow! That's really great. Where would you go though? Any plans for work?"

He was leading her. Working up some suggestion that would allow him to be close to her. The old 'let me take you out of here' schtick. A tired strip club regular trope. Easy enough to skirt when sitting in a velour lined VIP lap dance booth, not so much at a fancy Italian restaurant. Even worse now that she was unemployed and possibly unemployable.

"Not yet," she sipped her wine as she thought of what to say. "Honestly, I'm just not sure. I have a few ideas…." she lied, "But not totally sure. I've worked so long and losing my job, plus the death of my father kind of threw me off." One more sip, "I think I'd like to travel a bit and sort it out after I sell the property."

Pete's eyes sparkled. Fuck.

"Well, how about you give me the address? I'll have my realtor look up the comps and make an offer. Perhaps a generous one…I have a few investments I can liquidate." His eyes practically glittered, and she knew what was coming next. "Then I'll take you to Europe. We'll see a castle or two."

Fuckity, fuckity, fuck, she had at some point told him her dream of seeing a real castle someday. She still did. But not with Pete.

"That sounds fabulous!" She tried to put the glitter in her own eyes. She could cash the check for the house and tell him she broke her leg, or maybe simply fake her own death. Maybe the ethics of promising him she would go with him which pretty much implied she would fuck him, were a bit sketchy. But he did meet her in the strip club. Buyer beware. "I'll text you the address." She wasn't excited about giving him the address of her current residence, but she didn't have much of a choice. But he was excited at this new opening so she doubted he would fuck it up by showing up unannounced.

They finished dinner with light small talk, Pete practically glowing at the thought that he might finally be closing the deal. Not with the house, but with Georgia. She had to remind herself that their relationship was one of customer and entertainer, it had never been anything different. And she hadn't actually promised him anything. At least yet. It was just an implication of a deal.

Pete slid five crisp hundred-dollar bills into her hand as he walked her to her car. He hugged her, which she returned. But she turned her cheek when he went in for a kiss. His dry lips landed on her cheek instead of her mouth with enough force that was almost malicious. She drove home with her sunroof open so the night wind could dance in her hair. Rock music blaring as she turned down the driveway.

She was giddy as she walked up to her front door, but her smile faded as she reached for the knob. Something felt wrong. Off. Her smile melted when she turned the knob and found she didn't need her key. Her smile returned as she gripped the paper sack full of marijuana. She smoked a lot of weed. It made all the sense in the world that she only thought she locked the door when she left.

She pushed open the door and walked into the foyer where she had left the light on. A slight draft tickled her face as she walked deeper into the house and toward the back sliding door that led to the back deck. The door stood open. She wasn't smiling as she told herself that she had forgotten to lock that too.

Georgia could feel the weight of the gun under the pillow next to her. She locked all the doors and windows and then double checked that the house was secure before getting into bed. Then she got up and checked again. Now she lay staring at the ceiling which she had watched, not fully awake, burst forth the maggot spewing phantom of her dead father. Ralph lay not totally unperturbed at the end of her bed. His weight restricting the movement of her feet but providing comfort instead of annoyance this time. His head rested on his front paws, but she could tell he wasn't sleeping. Of all the things on her mind, that Ralph didn't want to close his eyes bothered her the most. She should be drifting off to sleep on the wave of his tiny kitty snores. Instead, they both seemed to be waiting for the next shoe to drop.

She had the gun, she told herself. She wasn't going to win any shooting contests, but Georgia was reasonably certain that she could hit something or someone if she needed to. She wasn't scared, but raging pissed about it. She had tried and failed a thousand times as she looked up at the drywall over her bed to convince herself that she had left the back door not just unlocked but wide open. She might have succeeded if it weren't for the cat she never wanted, sleeping with one eye open at the end of the bed. She had read that animals could sense earthquakes and other phenomena. If she believed in ghosts, she would have probably told herself that's what it was. She assumed that if ghosts were real their incorporeal bodies wouldn't be much of a physical threat. Her cat could be simply sensing a spirit or some other unseen but likely innocuous thing, and that she had the memory of a pot smoking goldfish that had forgotten to shut and lock her doors. If she could only convince herself of that, she might already be sleeping. But that wasn't it. Her memory was trash, and ghosts aren't real, and her damned cat was afraid of a real live human. One that had broken into her home.

She heard whispers. Or thought she heard whispers. Faint moaning. She listened carefully. Leaves brushing on the roof. Or maybe the window? She held her breath and listened. It sounded like it was coming from the attic. And it was a voice. Or words of some sort. Repeating. Although, she couldn't make out what they were saying.

She got up. She had already searched the place, twice, for anything amiss. There was nothing out of place. Nothing at all. Georgia was happy that whoever, was fucking with her had decided against animal cruelty this time. She couldn't help but be at least a little grateful for that. It could've been Ralph. The fucking bastards. Someone or some people just wanted her to know they got in. That was enough.

But she hadn't bothered to search the attic, and Eric had only scanned it with the flashlight after the ghost incident. It was easy to forget it even existed now that it was empty. Or at least she had succeeded in convincing herself it was just a storage place for holiday decorations. With her gun pulling down the band of her panties and the handle of a small flashlight in her mouth, she pulled down the ladder and climbed up. Her first thought was to check the place right above her bedroom. It paid off immediately. A small digital player sat right above not just her bedroom, but her bed. As she held it in her hand, it played. The sound of human voices. Mostly indistinct sounds, but she thought she heard the word Satan. She flipped it over and checked the settings. It was set to be repeated but at intervals. Whoever had been in her house tonight hadn't left it. It had been here before. When Eric had heard it and been inspired to buy the sage bundle. Which meant that they had been in the house before. She didn't bother getting back in bed.

In the short time she had been there, she still hadn't hooked up cable or internet and didn't see any reason to unpack her small laptop. She didn't use it much anyway, but she now pulled it out, booted it up and connected it to her phone's hotspot. She started with just a search of the word haunted and the house address. As the results appeared, it occurred to her that she hadn't ever wondered about the history of her dad's house. No real reason to. Growing up in Blackberry Ridge, she learned of its history as a mining and farming town. But it wasn't one of the famous gold rush towns kids might learn about in school. More like one that popped up by proxy. Just a blip in a much larger story. Blackberry Ridge had fostered only resentment not curiosity or pride in her as other small towns might instill in the kids that grew up there. The truth was she had just never given a shit. She still wasn't sure if she gave a shit, but she thought it might be worth at least a small turd to do a bit of research. She had so far done well in maintaining her apathy about her father and the town, but this was beginning to get scary. Blackberry Ridge was full of jerks, that didn't seem to need a reason to be jerks. This was a lot of trouble to go to just troll someone.

What she found was a ton of ghost hunter blogs. Because of course. That made sense. What many of the miners, settlers, and other residents of these places found wasn't gold, but death and disease and misery. Digging gold out of the dirt, ditches, and breaking it free of the quartz wasn't easy. But it only took one or two to get lucky before scores of hapless gullible fools bet their lives on finding the same fortune. While those who sold the dream and the supplies were the ones who got rich. And when it was all over, the tragedies real or imagined became a gold mine in themselves for the bloggers selling their own gold pans full of bullshit. To the Berry Folk's credit, they had so far succeeded in fending off the grifters and trolls with their EMF readers and exaggerated TikTok jump scares from invading their town.

On the surface, there didn't seem to be much of a story beyond the rumors. But as she continued to pull the thread of the specific area where her property was located, things got a little sketchy. She found only one blog that specifically mentioned her father's house.

The short blog on 'The Haunted Skeptic,' she couldn't help but roll her eyes at the name as this dude was neither a skeptic nor haunted, stated that the property was rumored to be sitting on an old cemetery and once had a gold claim. So, basically the plot of Poltergeist, but gold rush style. She rolled her eyes. The story was vague and full of worn-out stereotypes and neither helpful nor interesting nor all that imaginative. But the story of the death of a nearby was. The guy was hanged. But that wasn't the interesting part. He was hanged for his involvement in the occult. Namely, secret satanic gatherings. According to the blogger, the satanic stuff also involved animals and while not specifically mentioned but instead just inferred, human sacrifice. The 'ol Satanic Panic reboot. Also, pathetically unimaginative.

A few wayward miners thought they could increase their luck by appealing to Satan, which she wouldn't find surprising if true, given the superstitious and religious practices at the time, according to the blogger at least. The Haunted Skeptic had come to believe that Ron's property contained the spirit of the

Satanist. His reasoning was based on the rumors of someone he had spoken to in the town of Blackberry Ridge whose name he refused to reveal to protect their privacy. Because privacy according to this guy was only important in protecting a town gossiper, and not the actual resident of the property.

"This guy is a real doucher," she said to Ralph, who had followed her from her bedroom. He now laid on the sofa and watched as she searched the internet at the small dining table.

She looked for any other verification of the hanged thief or the ritualist gatherings he was supposed to have had and found exactly nothing. No name, no other rumors. Nothing. But the story was consistent with the rumors about her dad and the property. She decided she would dig into the story a little deeper than google to see if the stories of ghosts and satanic shit had any origins outside of Blackberry Ridge. But for now, she felt safe in assuming they came from the town itself. Or the imagination of a want to be ghost hunter who grew up in the 80s where every heavy metal fan or Dungeons and Dragons player was really worshipping the Devil. Satan, Satan everywhere.

Georgia began to fight her eyelids, but she was curious about the guy from the blog. Most ghost stories are recounted several times by several people. The more a story, whether true or not gets repeated the more credibility it appears to have, and she had seen that with multiple stories about the area she was looking at. Typical stuff about murdered prostitutes, minors driven crazy by syphilis, and one almost cute but still disturbing story about a little kid that liked to pull the skirts of women because they missed their mother. But the story about her father's house specifically, had only come from this one blog. This one guy, who apparently worked alone, had only a few other posts, which struck her as a little strange. All his posts were dated within a week of each other. So, dude decided he wanted to be a ghost hunter and started a blog, then gave up after a week or so. The cement block that sat in her gut told her this meant something. But even her tired brain knew better than to assume. But she did want to know a little more about The Haunted Skeptic, aka Tyler Johnson, before she gave up the ghost and try to get back to sleep.

She searched his name and came up with somewhere in the realm of a hundred and a thousand results. She frowned and tried again using the state he said he was from, with pretty much the same result. She went back to the blog and looked at the bio picture. A smiling guy with one eyebrow raised under a shaggy cut in a black and white selfie. His age was hard to determine, but she was thinking mid-twenties to late thirties. She began to look for the guy in social media pages with the name and found nothing. Finally, she searched for the photo itself, feeling a little dumb she hadn't done that at first.

The photo came back to a stock photo site. The cement liquified.

Georgia took a deep breath. So what? Some wannabe ghost hunter didn't want to use his own picture on a blog he ran for a week or two and gave up on it.

"It just feels wrong," she said to Ralph, who ignored her from the couch.

It was nearly three a.m., and the cement in her stomach migrated upward to her eyelids. A wall of fuzzy cobwebs creeped through her thoughts, and she closed the computer. She thought she saw a shadow lurking outside the large picture window, but that was only a trick of her tired eyes. Her thoughts drifted to Eric, and she found she no longer wanted to think about satanic ghost stories and dead miners. Ralph didn't fully wake as she picked him up and placed him at the foot of the bed, wondering if she would lie awake again or if she might be graced with another maggot-filled waking nightmare. Wouldn't that be a treat? But she barely set her head down before there was only darkness.

The text notification shocked her awake, drenched in sweat. There wasn't a dream she remembered, but night sweats didn't require one. They were a gift all on their own. She opened her eyes and picked up her phone. The time read ten am, the text was from Pete.

Hey you! My realtor ran the comps. I'm in. Let's meet up again. I got to get up there and take a look, but I'm ready to start the process. I can be up there this afternoon.

She replied, *Omg! That's great. Today isn't good though, let me get back to you.*

She put her phone back down and rolled onto her back and fell back asleep.

When she woke again, it was to the sound of Eric, knocking gently and not at all cop-like at her door.

18

PLAY IT COOL, she told herself as she opened the door. Then leapt into his arms. He carried her naked back into her bed, where they didn't make love. They fucked like animals. He followed her into the shower, where they continued before finally using the shower for its intended purpose. She didn't end up playing it cool, but she did play it honest. With Eric, she could drop her mask, and that felt almost better than the sex. Almost.

"I brought some stuff," Eric said as he pulled on his pants.

"Oh yeah?"

"Yeah, I figured I'd stop and grab some supplies."

"Ouija board, magic candles, crystals charged with moonbeam energy...?" Georgia said with an eyebrow that raised more easily than she thought ideal.

"Nope. But food. I figured this way we wouldn't have to go to the store."

She followed him out to the car and helped him carry in a few bags and a small cooler containing the cold stuff. He recounted all the current gossip and drama from the club as she made them French toast, fruit, and coffee. It was early afternoon, but morning to those that worked the night shifts.

"Wow. That's crazy," although it was all pretty normal if she were being honest. Money sucked, as it usually did as fall bled into winter. He gave her the dirty details about how Angel got fired. Apparently, she didn't steal from another girl, but from the bartender's tip jar. They had her on camera. She was lucky she hadn't been tarred and feathered. Georgia couldn't hide her glee at that.

She wasn't happy to hear that one of her friends, Coco had gotten into a fight. Over a song, because of course. Seemed like a silly thing to get in a fist fight over, even though Georgia understood exactly why it happened. Strippers get attached to songs, they absorb them into their identity. What song you danced to on stage didn't have that big of an impact on the customers, really, but they greatly influence how a stripper feels on stage. And like everything in the strip club, whether a song belonged to someone was a matter of how much they tipped the DJ. Coco had been out-tipped. Usually this kind of thing didn't end up in a physical fight, but well...Georgia knew it wasn't water in Coco's water bottle, and she had a tendency to get a little extra spicy as the night went on. But at least she had only been suspended and not fired.

As he cleared their plates, she told him about cleaning out the shed and putting the uninvestigated contents in the bed of the truck. She left out the part about the bear trap and other things that would make him worry. He was here now, and she didn't think anyone would be trying to break in with him there.

Eric typed something on his phone and said, "I texted Ken. I know he's got a buddy with a junk yard. I think he can have someone come take it away."

"Oh yeah, he still owe you a favor?" She said with a smirk, only half joking. Strip club owners, at least to her knowledge, didn't generally do things out of the goodness of their hearts.

And Ken had already let him out of a bunch of shifts. With pay. Which was only weird if she thought too much about it, which she made a point not to.

"Sure." His curt tone brought a single squirming maggot to the French toast in her stomach. His tone told her she probably didn't want to know anymore. "I unloaded those tools by the way, Larry was stoked."

"Larry?"

"Yeah, you know. Tall dude, electrician."

"Oh yeah, always dirty and always broke," for a guy that almost never had money for lap dances, and when he did, he always got a crappy one because of his sketchy personal hygiene, she actually kind of liked Larry. His unshaking optimism in spite of his equally unshakeable BO, was somehow endearing.

"Anyway, here you go," Eric pulled several hundred dollar bills out of his wallet.

"Sweet, but you can keep that. Just get rid of the truck."

"Don't you need it?"

He meant the money not the truck, she definitely didn't need that. She didn't want to tell him about Pete, but felt like it was kind of inevitable that he would find out. Eric wasn't going to be jealous, that would be silly, but he might question her safety. Or judgement. Which would be worse.

"I'm good actually...You remember Pete?"

"Your Tuesday night regular? Yeah." Again, she wasn't excited about his tone.

"I think he's going to buy the house," she paused, but remembered she was a big girl that could take care of herself. "I met him for dinner last night, he gave me some cash. I gave him the address to check the property values."

Eric's eyes darkened. she held her breath. How he handled this information might make or break whatever they had here, "Ok, as long as you trust him."

"I mean, I can't imagine dude would come up here to murder me. I've known the guy for over a decade. Besides, it simply solves another problem."

"Can't say I can find an argument there."

Her body relaxed as her heart swelled. Benevolent sexism wasn't going to be a thing with him. "He texted this morning that he's ready to talk numbers."

"That's cool."

"Right? If it works out, it will be much easier than having to go through a realtor and all that. Hoping he'll just cut a check and we'll...I'll be done with it." The promise of the trip to Europe could make it a bit more complicated than that, but nothing she couldn't handle. It was just part of the fantasy she had created for him. "By the way, I checked out some stuff about this place online last night. Some ghost hunter wrote up a blog about the place..."

"Ha! Told ya!"

"No dude. It was obviously crap. The guy used a stock photo. And the whole story came from an 'anonymous source from Blackberry Ridge.' In other words, some dickhead from Blackberry Ridge made a fake blog about a fake ghost story. It involved Satanic rituals and the ghost of a miner. Which I'm thinking explains the mannequins at least. I think my dad was trying to ward off the spirit or something. The spirit that he believed in because someone was making him think he was seeing shit. Or fuck, maybe he was seeing shit his own brain was manufacturing." She locked eyes with him as she reached into her pocket and pulled out the tiny player. "I found your ghost by the way." She tossed it in his direction, and he caught it midair.

"Where did you find that?"

"In the attic above the bedroom. So not a ghost. Just a dickhead from Blackberry Ridge," or dickheads. She suspected a team effort here, but he could figure that out on his own.

"Well, that dickhead planted that here." He crinkled his forehead and it reminded her that she would be ready for another injection soon. Now that he knew that the ghost wasn't real, and that someone had come on to the property, she thought she was going to have to tell him the rest. And she might have to admit, she didn't really want to be alone until she figured this out. "Do you have any idea why?" He was making her not wanting a relationship really hard.

"Not really, but I was thinking we could head to the county library or something and do some real research. Mainly on the property itself. Maybe that will give us the why."

"Your dad was a Christian right? Did he switch sides?"

"Who fucking knows? Satan and God are just stories so I'm thinking the rules are pretty subjective. And while he wasn't babbling in the streets, I'm thinking that he might have lost track of a few of his marbles. He was probably very suggestable. But before I dump this place off to Pete, I'd like to know. Or at least figure out who wants us to believe the house is haunted."

"The dickhead in the ghost get-up and the player in the attic aren't the only times someone has been here...?"

She sighed, "Come on, I'll tell you in the car. Just promise you won't freak out."

"I can't promise something like that," he smiled.

As they drove toward the small but bigger town which housed the county buildings, including the library, she told him everything. The raccoon, how the realtor was supposed to be Beth but was really her old high school bully Ann. The door she had found unlocked and the back door wide open. Why she didn't inspect any of the contents of the bins. He listened but said nothing. Until she got to the bear trap. By then they had pulled up to the county library. An old stone building in the county seat, looking very much like the heart of its own wicked ghost story.

"Oooo...that's pretty brutal. But I guess if we hear screaming, we won't think it's a ghost."

"You mean *you* won't think it's a ghost. I watched enough Scooby Doo to know it's always just some greedy old dude in a mask."

Her phone pinged. "Fuck. It's Pete. I forgot to get back to him about coming up to look at the place."

"Perfect, now you won't be there by yourself when he comes up." When he saw the look on her face he continued, "I mean I'll be in the shed or something. Just in case." If Pete knew that Georgia had a boyfriend, it could dispel the fantasy and thereby sour the deal.

"Thank you," she said with her eyes glued to stone building, "I'm going to tell him to come up tomorrow. How long are you going to stay by the way?"

"As long as I want. Cashed in my PTO."

"Ha! PTO," was her reply. She had never heard of paid time off at the strip club. Her phone pinged again. "Ok, tomorrow at 1 pm."

The cold grey stone steps that led up to the heavy double doors were cracked and chipped by a hundred and fifty years of feet stamping up and down them. Inside was just as cold and but was warmed by an exuberant fire in the main reading room fireplace. Above the mantle, an old man depicted in ancient oil paint stared at them.

"Oh yeah, that dude is definitely knocking on walls and rattling chains at three a.m.," Eric whispered.

He was just talking, but Georgia was willing to bet, there was a ghost story that told exactly that. If her memory was correct, which it could very well not be, that dude in the painting was one of the first people to strike gold. Kicking off the rush that for most part, had been a fool's errand.

At the mahogany counter, an old lady who looked to be just about dead herself looked at them as a smile cracked her face and asked if she could help them. Georgia asked for the records room, and the old lady motioned for them to follow her down an enormous hallway. She showed them where they could find the property records and old news articles.

"Ha! Microfiche! I didn't think that was a thing anymore," Eric said, forgetting to whisper. The librarian shushed him with just a dirty look as she left them alone.

"I didn't either," Georgia said in an exaggerated whisper.

It took both of them a few minutes to figure out just how to use the old equipment, but once they did, Eric took the property records and Georgia started to look at the old news stuff. In minutes, Eric tapped her on the shoulder.

"Dude. Look at this. Your dad built the house. Did you know that?"

"I didn't. My mother never really spoke about it. I meant to ask, but never did."

"Wait, you didn't know anything about your family at all?"

"I really didn't. My mother's parents were gone before I was born, and she lived with her aunt, but she died when I was little. I knew exactly fuck all about my dad and his family. It wasn't up for discussion. So, I didn't ask. Especially not as a kid. My mom said it wasn't anything to worry about."

"Well, it looks like he inherited the land and built the house on it. It goes all the way back to the first settlers here."

"No sign of a cemetery, or Satan?" she said sarcasm bleeding into her voice.

"Nope, just old mining land." He scrolled, "But look at this. There was a gold claim on the property."

"Huh…" she thought of the hole in the dirt floor of the shed. She hadn't mentioned that part to him, mostly because she had been trying to forget about it. "So, in the shed, there's a piece of plywood covering a hole. It's probably nothing. I'm sure it's nothing, there are a ton of old mines up there. All totally worthless or too hard to excavate."

"Do you think it's an old mine?"

"I don't think it's impossible. But that doesn't mean there's gold in there. There are abandoned mines all over the area. A lot of them sprung up from rumors or even deliberate lies meant to mislead people away from where the actual deposits were. Although, I have heard but can't remember how true it is, that only 10% of the gold was actually removed. It's all laced in the quartz and rocks and super hard and expensive to get to. So just because you find a little, doesn't mean you can practically get enough to mean anything. Like winning five bucks on a dollar scratcher, that makes you buy more but then you never win again."

"Wow, check out the big brain on the stripper..."

"Ex-stripper. I know my brain is big, but have you seen my boobs?" Georgia grinned, "I read a lot as kid. Is there anything else?"

"A title record placing the house and property into a trust."

"Yeah, to me, right?"

"Yup," he squinted to read the tiny blurry print, "Looks like he used an estate lawyer....Bradley Realty."

"Cunt!" Georgia forgot to whisper.

"I'll get to that later," he smiled, "What's up?"

"Ann Bradley was the realtor I punched in the face."

"I'm sure she deserved it."

"She did, but when I called to set up the meeting she was going by Beth." Georgia looked at the date, "That was right after my mom and sister died. Not long after I moved out."

Eric looking out the window at the orange and red leaves on the monster sized trees in the old parking lot, asked "How did you find the realtor?"

"It was with the stuff the lawyer gave me. I asked her for a reference actually." She paused, "Fuck me, the estate lawyer was from Blackberry Ridge and also apparently from Bradley Realty. Maybe I should have punched her in the face too."

"There is still time."

"Which is right around the time the Satan stuff started."

"You think Ann started the Satanic Panic of Blackberry Ridge?"

"A strong maybe. It coincides with the blog. My dad was always the subject of shit talking, but mostly for being a recluse. For small town rumors, Satan isn't much of a stretch."

Eric forgot to whisper again, "Ann is the greedy old man in the mask?"

"Shhhh......!" The old lady materialized out of nowhere.

"Fuck!" Georgia and Eric said in unison.

Georgia caught herself and said with as much calm and politeness as she could muster, "Oh. We're so sorry. We'll be quiet."

The librarian gave them a look from beyond the near grave and floated back out.

"Hey, you remember the library scene from Ghostbusters?"

She rolled her eyes and giggled.

"Ok, so roll with me here," Georgia said, exaggerating her whisper, "What if Ann, thought there was gold hidden on the property and started all this shit to get her hands on it? Drove him nutty, or nuttier in hopes she could get it? Fake website planted rumors. He would've been such an easy target. The town pariah already. It wouldn't be hard to get the town to believe even more bullshit."

"What if there *is* gold on the property?"

"We got to look in the hole, don't we?"

"We do," he was smiling. "We might need to go through the stuff from the shed too."

"Let's start with the hole," it was her turn to smirk at the dirty pun. But it was the goofy jokes that distracted her from thinking about what might be in the hole. She didn't think it was gold.

Eric and Georgia stopped at a diner before heading down

the windy road that would take them to Blackberry Ridge. She had wanted to get back before dark, but that wasn't going to happen anyway, and a bit of comfort food couldn't be the worst idea.

"Ok, so kind of a shitty question. But I got to ask," Eric said as he stuck a hand cut golden french fry into his mouth. "The bod….er….stuff in the attic…" He didn't finish because the look on her face told him he didn't have to. He just watched and stuck another fry in his mouth as he waited for her to answer.

Georgia picked at her homemade chicken pot pie, twisting her fork around in the guts of it, "I don't fucking know. For real, I never thought the guy was dangerous. Or even particularly a bad guy. I mean, I still feel exactly fuck all when I think of him being dead. I might have seen him a few times a year, but there was no connection with him at all. I wonder now if he simply wasn't capable of it. A connection I mean. But it's still hard for me to think he was capable of….." her fork twisted again, "that." She finally stuck a forkful of her food in her mouth. It was delicious, but it sat on her tongue like a glob of coagulated glue. She forced it down. "But what other explanation could there be? It's not like someone hid them in the attic without him knowing about it."

Eric chewed his cheeseburger, then said, "Maybe they were accidents?"

"Come on. That doesn't make sense. What we know, or what it looks like at least, is that Ann came across this old gold claim. Decided getting the property from the town's nutty hermit, would be pretty easy. I bet if we were to trace back that stupid blog, we would find Ann. Or someone that knew her. Lending credit to the Satan shit and set to drive the guy even more crazy to get him to sell."

"Or die."

"Can't say that hasn't crossed my mind. But if there was any evidence of foul play, no one told me. He was found, and cremated, and I never picked up the ashes. He was old, didn't look like he was taking great care of himself. All alone with that stupid cat."

"You said the trust was created around when you mom and sister died. He wanted to make sure you had the place. He could've just sold it. Maybe the gold mine thing isn't so ridiculous."

Georgia looked down at the pale creamy lumpy meal she had ordered and pushed it away. The more she stared at it, the more it began to squirm. Maggots. If what Eric said was true, it meant that her dad had cared about her. Gold mine or not, she hadn't talked to him in so long, that he still thought about her at all, made the few bites of food in her stomach quiver.

"I can't say it isn't possible, but more people died up there for the promise of gold than actually found it. The accident really fucked him up. The last time I spoke with him he was screaming about the stop sign."

Eric having finished, pushed his own plate away, "Could Ann or her minions have had something to do with it." If she looked hard enough, she might have been able to see him cringe asking.

"It's possible he thought they were murdered, yes. But he wasn't dealing with a full deck. And the driver of the truck was seriously injured. I think the accident was just that. But I don't think it would be hard for him to think it wasn't. I also think that it might have been a great way to exploit his mental state for someone to make him think it was murder. Besides, if they had done something like that, why not me too?"

Georgia was watching this part of the conversation from a place just outside her mind. If she watched from the outside, she could avert the tears.

"Because you were already estranged from him as far as anyone might know right? You were already gone and out of the town."

"I suppose. But when Ann showed up, she played the nice

guy for all of five minutes, then started talking shit. Until I made her stop. You know? I think that was the first time I've ever hit anyone. If she were trying to get the property from me, why would she do that? She basically sabotaged her own effort. Maybe were on the wrong path here."

"Or maybe she didn't need to be nice to you."

"How would that work?" Georgia was getting as frustrated as she was nauseated.

"She found someone else to buy it for her."

"But no one else..." Georgia's pot pie flipped, "Pete?"

The check had come, and Eric grabbed it before she could, maybe benevolent sexism wasn't all that bad.

"Everyone knew you were a stripper, even not using your real name, there's only a couple of clubs in town."

"But how would she connect me to Pete? That seems a bit much," she frowned as they got up to leave.

"A well placed twenty in the hands of any stripper in the club could probably get pretty much any information one wanted," Eric said.

She just nodded as she opened his door with a valiant flourish.

"Pete wants to take me to Europe after he buys the house. I don't know. I have a hard time thinking he would do me dirty like that."

"You know the dude better than me but ask him who his realtor is tomorrow. If she had found out there was a connection between you guys, maybe she planted the seed. Primed him for the con."

Eric was making sense. Like a lot of sense. She didn't think Pete was an idiot, but his motivations weren't all that hard to figure out. He would be plenty malleable in the hands of an attractive woman. Not that Georgia thought that Ann was all that attractive, she thought she looked a bit like a troll, but she could see how she might be doable in the eyes of a desperately lonely guy.

"If he is working with Ann, I might just kick him in the balls."

"But who cares if he is? So, what if she gets the property? Especially if there is nothing there but an old empty mine? Or even if there is gold in the fucking mine. You want to pull it out? You think there's even enough to be worth the effort? You could just let her have it, and we can move on."

Again, he is making all sorts of sense. Why should she give a shit at all? She'd still get paid.

She focused on the unbroken yellow line on the road as it whizzed by in the dark. Her hands on the wheel followed it as she sped toward the house she didn't want. She had only ever wanted the money. There was no legacy, no history there. No memories with her father that she could keep alive there. She had memories, but the bad ones insisted on lingering like cheap cigar smoke. There was nothing. But that wasn't all the way true. A lot true but not all the way. That town. That small town community had a horrific dark side. It wasn't all farmers markets and fall festivals. It couldn't thrive without someone to hate, someone to pick out for ridicule. Its strength it's bond, was found by manufacturing a common enemy, in a troubled man. What she learned at the library had planted a seed. Maybe her dad hadn't killed those people? Maybe they had come to fuck with him? Or maybe they were meant to frame him for murder? Ann and her ilk made her life a living hell, for the sheer joy in it. Did she really want to let her win?

"Because fuck Ann Bradley, that's why." Georgia let up off the gas just a bit as she glided into a hairpin turn, then punched the gas on the way out. She didn't hear Eric suck in a terrified breath. "And fuck Blackberry Ridge."

19

HER ANGER FOLLOWED her to bed and was still with her when she woke up. Eric still snoring beside her, only Ralph got up with her to start the coffee. She took it out to the back porch and stared at her back yard as it melted into the woods. She screamed and dumped her coffee off the railing as Eric came up behind her.

"The fuck?" she said trying and failing to find anger at losing her coffee. "I guess I was done anyway."

"You ready to go mining for gold?"

"Yeah. Maybe. No." Georgia turned to face him. He took her face in his hands and kissed her deeply. When he let her go, she took his coffee and took a sip, locking eyes with him as she did. They stood there trading sips from the one mug, looking out into the country.

"You said last night that your dad was found and cremated and that you didn't know anything else. Do you know who found him?" Eric said, but didn't face her, just continued to look out into the yard.

Astounded that she never thought to ask. Georgia hadn't even thought much about her father since they last spoke. Years after that, she didn't miss him. There hadn't been anything to miss. She had been surprised to have been informed about his death at all. But not surprised at his death, or simply so apathetic to the circumstances of how he died it never even crossed her mind.

"I can't remember. If that isn't totally fucked up. They must have said right? And I just forgot?" Memory problems, hormones strike again.

"Are you sure they did tell you? Or was it in the paperwork? Police report? Something?" He was looking at her now.

"I didn't go through the paperwork. It was all handled. I just signed some stuff and took the key. I figured his death was old age, who might have found his body didn't seem relevant?" She was feeling a bit stupid at this point, "I guess it does now. Shit. But I think maybe the lawyer said it was a neighbor?"

"You still have all the paperwork?"

"Of course. I'm not totally stupid you know, just a little maybe."

"Nah. You didn't even know the guy really. Hated the town, so why would you give a shit?"

"You uh...saying I have daddy issues?"

"Well. Had," he only half smiled, unsure of how this joke would land. Pussy and dick and sex jokes were always cool, dead possibly murderous father jokes were a little sketchy.

"Fair point," she smiled and kissed him. But inside, she cringed a little. Georgia was alone for almost all of her adult life. Her father had become a shadow of memory. Like a mythical being from a time just outside her existence. The memories of her childhood lay behind an opaque wall, just shadows moving in some vaguely familiar way. Only the insults, laughing at her expense, the cruelty, ostracization, and abandonment blazed in white hot clarity. Those times she remembered perfectly. "I'll go get them."

Dumping her coffee, even though her favorite mug was

now in pieces on the other side of the railing, was the best thing that could have happened to Georgia's nerves. She had finished half of it but was vibrating anyway. She had kept a file box with her important paperwork in the spare bedroom, mostly empty except for her unpacked boxes and Ralph's litter box. Mostly dance contracts, tax stuff, and ID papers. She found the file given to her by her father's estate lawyer Shelley, also her former classmate, and current employee at Bradley Realty.

"Here it is," she said as she sat down in one of the deck chairs. Eric had replenished his coffee and gotten her a fresh cup. She looked at it but didn't pick it up. Instead, she just stared at the manilla folder in her lap. She took a deep breath, a deep sense of gratitude that she wasn't alone rode out with her outgoing breath. Gratitude she wasn't able to admit to herself, and certainly not to Eric, but was there just the same. She opened the folder and scanned each page before handing it to Eric.

"So, this all seems pretty normal. No creepy dude in a mask," he said. "Although, can't say I'm an expert in any of this."

"I mean I haven't ever done this stuff either. At least not like this. With my mom and sister, there wasn't really anything but tying up the loose ends," she did that thing where she was on the outside looking in. If she ever got her ass into therapy, they would probably tell her that disconnecting was a bad thing, and Georgia would tell them they were full of shit. "Oh, hey! Here's a copy of the gold claim."

Eric scanned it, "It is the same one I found at the library." He crinkled his forehead, "So riddle me this Batman...Ann wanted the property from your dad to get the gold claim, fucked with him, and planted the Satan stuff. But..."

"Why would she help facilitate putting the trust and stuff in my name? Could she just have had it put in her own?" She took the gold claim back and studied it, something bugged her about it but she didn't want to say that out loud. She moved on to the last document. "Here is the death certificate."

"So natural causes, Cardiac infa….heart attack, oh and methamphetamine. Shit, did you know…"

"If he used drugs? No, dude. I didn't know shit remember?" She took the certificate back from him. She looked again but held it a little farther away to read the fine print. "There says there was an autopsy performed, but I think the combo of meth and the fact that the dude seemed to be living off top ramen, kinda answers the death question. I still want to know who found him. Not thinking I want to ask Shelley."

"Shelley?"

"Sorry, the estate lawyer."

"Think there would be a police report?"

"You'd think." Georgia went back to the gold claim document. "So, here's the other thing that doesn't make sense, if they are after the property because they want the gold claim, why include it here? Why tell me that?"

"Have no idea. Maybe she had to include it by law? Disclosure or something? Either way, I think we need to go look in the shed. At least to be sure. But nothing at this point explains the…well, you know."

"Yeah, I fucking know. Let's go," Georgia didn't allow the relief she was feeling that whatever was in that hole, she wouldn't be finding it alone.

As Eric opened the doors to the shed, Georgia closed her eyes. She kept them closed as she heard him lift up the plywood sheet covering the hole in the dirt. Expecting a scream, or a wow, or an exclamation of some sort, but all she got was silence. She finally opened her eyes. A large dirt hole met her gaze. She stepped a little closer and looked down and saw more dirt.

"Oooo…..dirt." Eric said as he walked closer and peered down into it. "But there is something else."

Georgia cringed as she watched him reach down into the pit.

"It's a roach!" He smiled and held it up.

"Well, that's an easy one, I smoked that and dropped in the hole when I was cleaning it out."

Eric was staring down into the hole, as Georgia walked over to join him. "Can't say it looks like a mine. More like a huge gopher hole. Which totally tracks by the way. A ton of those around here."

"It looks like it was dug out with a shovel though," he said.

"What are you some sort of dirt hole expert?" She said with as much animosity she could spare, but then started laughing.

"Only if she's drunk enough!"

Georgia rolled her eyes but kept laughing. Before pulling a joint from the pocket of her sweatshirt. "Now we have to look in the bins, don't we?"

"We kind of do," he said as he pulled a lighter out of his own sweatshirt pocket. Georgia smiled slightly at the weird ying yang kind of romantic moment. They fit together like puzzle pieces. His flame to her ganja.

Eric pulled the plywood out of the shed and set it down next to the truck. He took the joint from Georgia and inhaled deeply before passing it back. She got the distinct impression that he was stalling also. And it only made her like, *love?* him more. They stood over the hole in the shed and passed the joint back and forth.

"Hey, I think there is something down here," Eric reached in and picked at the corner of what looked like paper. "I think..."

The sound of tires on gravel cam behind them, Georgia stepped out of the shed to see a large white truck coming down the driveway.

"Holy fuckballs! It's Pete. I totally forgot. Stay here," she said as she shut the shed doors.

20

<hr>

"Hi sweetie! So happy to see you. Oh my god, you look great!" Pete said ensnaring Georgia in a bear hug tight enough to rupture a lung.

"Ah, thanks," she said with her face smashed into his large over-cologned and flannel-ed chest. "I meant to change, sorry," suddenly very aware that she was in Georgia the person mode in her leggings and metal sweatshirt. Which could have been cute, if she had on her stripper face and her hair wasn't up in a messy bun. And not the kind that you see on Instagram, but the kind that you throw up when giving your guy a blowjob.

"Oh no, honey. You're gorgeous," he said, his words dripped with eager enthusiasm.

Enthusiasm which now seemed entirely too suspicious. She was pretty far from gorgeous at the moment. Pete had never seen her without her full get up he was either going blind or he was working with Ann. Georgia began to burn inside her sweatshirt, despite the crisp air. Sweat ran between her breasts and soaked into the waistband of her leggings. The fantasy was spoiled but his lust was not and that frightened her.

"Ah…thanks," she said as she extracted her face from his chest.

"So can I see the place?"

Georgia scolded herself inside her head for not remembering he was coming. She could have stopped him, but now he was here. And now she didn't trust him. She wasn't worried about her physical safety. Pete wasn't going try anything like that. He presumably was the good cop to Ann's bad one. Now she just wanted him to get the fuck out of the place. Maybe it wasn't gold they were after, but it was something. As she smiled at her long time Tuesday night regular, she was sure he was in on it.

"You know, I actually don't feel that good. I meant to text you, but I forgot. I know you came all this way, but can we do it another time?"

Pete's ruddy face darkened, "Oh, honey, I'm sorry. But hey the sooner we get this done, the sooner we can be in Europe." He winked and reached for her; she took a quick step back.

"Oh, shouldn't have hugged you already. That was terribly selfish of me, you don't want whatever this is."

"I'm a tough guy," he said, looking like a pinkish extra-large marshmallow stuffed into LL Bean red and black plaid that still smelled like the high-end department store it came from. He must have bought it on the way up there.

Not knowing what else to do other than tell him to get the fuck off her property, she said, "Ok, but for real. I feel like a warmed-over turd. Can we just take a quick look and then I need a nap. But we can do dinner again really soon and iron out all the details. Europe, here we come!" She impressed herself with her feigned excitement. An Oscar-worthy performance, if strippers could win Oscars. She had zero intention of selling to anyone until she figured out what was up.

Pete beamed his usual goofy smile and followed her up to the house.

She turned the knob and heard a loud deep growl as she pushed the door inward. A valiant Ralph sprung down from the top of the door, and onto Pete's face, ripping and tearing at his flesh. Blood soaked into his flannel as he screamed.

"Fuck," she said under her breath and opened the door for real. Pete followed her inside, where Ralph laid on the sofa. He jumped down when he saw Pete and ran into the spare bedroom. He hadn't done that with Eric.

Pete oooo'd and aaaah'd as she showed him the kitchen and back porch, the small dining room and front and spare bedroom. Ralph eyed Pete suspiciously from his thankfully clean litter box. Why that was his safe place, Georgia could only guess. She took him to the master bathroom where on the counter were two toothbrushes in the holder.

"Ha! Is the other one for the cat? Or are you cheating on me?" He said, wearing his goofy smile again but with way too many teeth.

Cheating? Pete wasn't just waving a red flag but stuffing it in her face. She had intended to gloss over the comment, but her mouth didn't want to cooperate with her brain.

"Cheating? We'd have to be a thing first," *Fuck, fuck, fuck*. Her mask slipped. She tried to fix it with an 'I'm only playing with you look.' "Of course it's for Ralph silly. Have you seen veterinary dental bills? I'm unemployed, remember?" She showed him her teeth in yet another hopefully award-winning smile.

"Those boots his, too?" Pete was looking at Eric's boots next to floor, right next to his discarded red boxer shorts. He moved closer to her next to her unmade bed. "It's okay. I know how you can make it up to me."

He swept her up in his arms and put two meaty hands on her ass. Her arms were pinned to her chest, and she wasn't able to take a full breath. Pete began to plant moist kisses on her face despite his dry thin lips. She tried to extend her arms out and push him away, but he only held her more tightly. One hand left her ass and crept up under her sweatshirt to where her breast was smashed against her own arm. Pete was giggling as if it were a game.

Playing into the game for fear of risking him becoming angry and more aggressive she said, laughing with him, "Hey, stop, you don't want to catch my sick."

"Maybe I want your sick," he said. Pushing her away and down onto the bed, letting her go as he did. "And you owe me. You didn't think that cash was just for the privilege of taking your teasing ass to dinner?"

She bounced herself right back up and he caught her, but this time flipping her around, so he had her from behind. He groped her breasts, something he had done in the club a million times. But this was different. This was dangerous. At any given time in the strip club, she would have five or six hundred pounds of bouncers standing behind her, now all she had was a DJ locked in her shed where he probably wouldn't hear her scream. What she did have was a gun.

When Eric wasn't there, her gun lived under the pillow. But she hadn't told him she had it, didn't want him to be all 'You sure you know how to use that?' or 'I thought you weren't scared'. So, she had slipped it between the mattress and boxspring to hide while he was there. With Pete's hands occupied, she stuck her hand under the mattress bending forward and pushing her ass farther against his groin. She swept her hand back and forth, as he grunted and pressed harder against her. She struggled to keep her panic from overtaking her as she felt only cool cloth covering the springs of the box spring. She felt her gorge rise, but then she felt the gun. She pulled it out and dove forward onto the bed, slipping out of his hands.

"Hey, sorry. I thought...wait..." Pete's eyes were double moons in the middle of his face.

"You thought what, motherfucker?"

Georgia had the gun pointed at his heart. She hoped her aim would hold true. She pulled the trigger.

A loud bang, then a red dot appeared in Pete's forehead. His eyes widened impossibly as he fell backward. Georgia gripped the gun harder as she heard the front door burst open.

"George! George!" Eric said. "Are you alright?" He tripped over Pete's head as he ran into the room but caught himself before he could fall forward. A move that would have been comical had it not been for the dead body in the room.

"I'm good," she said as wave of heat spread from her chest down to her knees.

21

She didn't drop the gun but set it gently on the bed. There was no point in checking to see if Pete was okay. He wasn't. Unless there turned out to be an afterlife. And if Pete had been a pretty decent guy, maybe his soul was in Heaven with angel strippers and never-ending plates of pasta. But in the here and now he was dead on the floor. No blood came out the back of his head.

"I think the bullet stayed in there," Georgia whispered.

Eric sat next to her on the bed, put his arms around her and said nothing.

"I really didn't think he was dangerous," she said with the full realization that what had likely fueled her assessment was the fact that she had never been around the guy without being on camera or without large aggressive men waiting for the opportunity to open the front door with some guy's head. "But he *wasn't* just playing."

Eric still said nothing but pulled away and took out his phone.

"You're calling the police?" Georgia said, although she was sure he was.

"No," he said and sent a quick text instead, then put his

phone back in his pocket. He got up off the bed and began to search Pete's pockets. As he did, he said, "That fucker had it coming. You didn't do anything wrong George." Eric probed every pocket on Pete's shirt and jeans and came away with only his keys.

"Is that why you're not calling the police?"

"We both know why I'm not calling the police," he held up the keys.

Of course, she knew why. The same reason she hadn't called the police every other time any sane rational person would have. She might not be a hooker, but she was still a sex worker. In the club she was an entertainer or performer. Out of it, she was a slut, whore, stripper and druggie grifter. Even if it all came out okay in the end and it were deemed self-defense, she'd go through hell to get there. And she'd need the pope himself to defend her. Nope. Police weren't an option. Her bravado, her once thought to be near supernatural stripper sense at being able to tell the bad from the good ones, had failed. She knew better than to give Pete her address. Her power and strength were an illusion in the strip club. She was but a little yapping chihuahua certain of her own power, totally unaware of the pit bull that stood behind her ready to eat the face off of anyone who tried to hurt her. She wasn't an expert at judging guys, she was just really good about tipping her security. This time the power had been hers. She had saved herself. But a bigoted country bumpkin cop could take it away from her. Her sense of power drained as she realized the danger she was in. Not from an overzealous customer, but from the not so blind eyes of the law.

Eric, with Pete's keys in his hands, kissed her on the forehead, then took her face in his hands, the black key fob dangling against her cheek. "Look, this is already handled. I promise."

"Okay," was all she said. Looks like he would be her knight in shining cotton whether she liked it or not. Her control slid out of her out of her hands and into his. Like she was drowning, and having nothing left to give she just let go and gave in. "What do I need to do?"

He paused, "You need to help me get him to the shed."

She left the gun on the bed, as she stood up. Pete lay with his head just inside the doorway. Ralph just stared at them from the hallway as they walked around the large body. He followed them down the hall but turned in the way of the kitchen as they walked toward the back deck. She diverted and filled his dish before joining Eric on the porch.

"Do you have a large sheet or blanket you can spare?" Eric asked quietly, seemingly unsure of how she was coping.

"I do. But does it matter?"

"I guess not. Fuck it..." he paused as if he had something else to say.

"You are wondering if I'm, okay?" Reading the pause. "I am. I think. Maybe I'll freak out later. Or not. Honestly, I think I'm becoming desensitized to all this bullshit." At least for now she felt that way, but she thought that therapy could be in her future. Although, how does one work through the murders her father committed, and the one she committed herself with a therapist? She knew there must be some kind of disclosure law for murder. Even one clearly committed in self-defense. She could always just take up drinking or something.

"It was self-defense, George. You know that don't you?"

"Do *you*?" She needed to know he didn't doubt her.

"I do. I was watching the whole thing. Sorry, but I wasn't going to chill in the shed." Part of her wanted to be super mad at him for not trusting her. Her emotions were the tangled mess of a multiple freeway junction where the signs had all been removed. All curves and twists with no real way to discern which ramp led where "You can obviously take care of yourself. I hope you understand that. But if he really is involved in all...

this…whatever it is, he wasn't just a normal strip club customer."

"I know. I get it," and she thought she did. "It's that I don't want you to wonder if I shot him because he was working with Ann and not because he was…well you know. It's not like he hasn't felt me up before with my permission if not my blessing."

"That means exactly shit, George, and I really hope you know that too. Let's say for just a second that he was only playing and wouldn't have gone any farther, you weren't in the club, and that wasn't okay. Full stop. Now if you shot him because he was working with Ann, then he was likely trying to hurt you for real. Either way, I think you were justified in ending that fuckwit." What he didn't say was that the cops probably wouldn't think she had been justified. Pete lying dead on the floor looked like every bit the victim.

Eric's phone rang, he took it out of his pocket and went inside speaking quietly. She was now alone on the porch. Ralph joined her, announcing his presence with a tiny meow. She sat down and he jumped into her lap. She pet him and stared out into the cool calm afternoon, wondering just how fucked up all this had gotten. She couldn't believe that at one point she thought that two dead bodies in her father's attic were about the worst it could get. She knew that even if the police thought it was self-defense, they would still find a way to make it her fault. That somehow Pete assaulting her was something that she had brought on to herself. Which was bullshit, but that's how these things go in these cases. She bet the first question they would ask her would be "What were you wearing?"

"Ok, you good?" Eric said as he came back outside.

"I am as good as I can be. Let's get this done."

Eric kneeled in front her, so he was face to face with Ralph, but looking up at her, "Do you believe me when I tell you that it's all going to be okay? Because it is."

"I want to," and she really did want to believe it was all going to be.

"You're not alone in this, George. You know that too, right?"

"I do, and that what fucking scares me the most."

"I know, but that's going to be okay too."

Ralph became annoyed as they kissed and hopped off her lap to take his place again on the sofa, where a now plump cat dent was forming. They went inside and said nothing to each other. Eric stepped over the body and plucked the gun from the bed. He wiped it off with his shirt, as he tucked into the waistband of the dead man on the floor. He hooked his arms under Pete's arm pits. Georgia tucked each ankle of the cooling corpse under her own arms, tightened her abs and focused her attention to her glutes and thighs. The last thing she needed was a sciatic attack. They lifted at the same time, Pete's ass sagged toward the floor, but they managed to keep it from touching as they walked him toward the front door, Eric taking small steps backward.

Eric had left the front door open, but they had to twist the body slightly to get it through. Georgia hadn't realized just how big he was. At least until she had to carry his body out to her father's old work shed. They set Pete down, as Eric opened the door to the shed. He then dragged the body the rest of the way in and shut the door. As he did, she noticed a white piece of paper sticking out of Eric's back pocket. She wasn't sure if she should ask about it, she was sure she didn't want to ask about the phone call. She decided he would tell her if she needed to know, and let it go as something else occurred to her.

"So, I feel kinda dumb not saying this before," she said as Eric stepped out of the shed and shut the doors. "But do you think that someone could be watching the house?"

Eric thought, then a slight wrinkle appeared in his forehead, "Yeah, I think that is a strong possibility. But if it helps, I feel kind of dumb about that too. So, we can be dumb together."

"Great, just a couple of dummies covering up a few murders.

I can't imagine whoever might be watching would go the police though. They probably have as much if not more than us to lose right?"

He reached for her and drew her close, "You're right. There is some shady shit going on here and has been for a while. If someone wanted heat, I think they would have already brought it." He took a small step backward and put his hand to his back pocket. "I have a joint….Oh wait. Shit. I totally forgot. Eric pulled the paper out of his back pocket. "This is for you."

He handed her a white envelope with a brown burn mark in the center of her handwritten name. It read 'G***gia.'

22

BEFORE COMING BACK UP to the house, Eric moved Pete's truck down the road and away from the property. Georgia didn't ask where. He had pulled out a pair of latex gloves from his car. Georgia didn't comment on them. She did ask if he had found anything in the truck that might connect him to Ann, and he said he didn't. No realtor cards or pamphlets. Pete's phone had a pin lock that Eric figured out easily on the first try, as it was 1234. But found no connection to Ann or the town either. No phone calls, texts or emails, from Ann or any other realtor. Pete had come up with the intention of attacking her.

Georgia turned the letter from her father over in her hand. She wished it sparked a feeling, any feeling other than dread. She even dared to hope it wasn't from him at all, maybe planted by the bastards who were currently making her life a waking nightmare.

"What if it's not from him?" She asked Eric as they sat on the porch with the opened letter.

"I don't know, either way it could give us some more insight to what is going on. Do you have any writing samples that we could compare it to?"

"I got to have something, but right now I can't think of any. I never saved anything, which would have been mostly Christmas cards anyway. But I threw those away," she said as she opened the letter. "Welp, never mind. It's typed." She scanned the page of unbroken sentences.

She read it aloud,

"Dear Georgia, I don't know if or when you'll find this. But if you do, I'm probably dead. Mike told me not to write this, and I wasn't going to, but the spirits compelled me. The good spirits. There are bad ones too. Mike and the spirits always agree, except for this. But that's why I hid it in the gopher hole in the shed. Never did find the gopher, dug out thing until it was easier to cover it up than fill it in. Ha Ha. There was no gopher. Except for me. I was the gopher. But I told Mike it was a gopher hole. Also, why I went to the library to type it out. Mike is a good guy, my friend. But he scares me when he gets mad. He scares Ralph too, although he gave him to me. I hope you are taking care of him. He's a good boy. A really good boy. Mike knows what to feed him. Ask him. He is still at the feed store. Has a wife and kid now. I can't remember if you liked Mike or not. I have so much to say but I don't know where to start, my thoughts come so fast these days and sometimes I wonder if they make sense. I know they do, but I don't think my words come out right all the time. People look at me funny. That's why I don't talk to people anymore, other than Mike. I used to talk to my friends in the attic, but now they have demons in them. My heart beats so fast sometimes. But Mike says that's from the good spirits. He has been bringing special herbs that have been helping. They help so much Georgia. I take them and feel like I'm flying. But then the spirits come. And they were nice at first but now they're mean. Mike says they're angry. Mike says they might come to hurt you. Or Ralph even. I know they want to hurt me. He helped me gather my friends in the attic, they have been keeping you safe Georgia. Mike brought them to me, and we trapped a demon in each one. Then every full moon, I gather with them, and we pray to keep the demon inside. If you find them, Georgia, you must burn them because I can't. The one who put them there can't send them back to Hell. I know you don't believe in this stuff Georgia but it's true. I'm sorry to leave you this burden, but Mike said that they killed your mom and sister. I am hiding from them. Mike gave me a spell that keeps them out of the attic. I live there now. I made the house nice for you though. Once the demons are gone you can live there." She paused, taking a breath.

"Does that sound like him?" Eric asked.

"It does, fuck. He was barely coherent when I spoke to him last. Frantic. But I'm pretty sure this is him. He talked fast and moved from subject to subject the last few times I talked to him. Now I'm thinking that the *herbs* Mike was giving him probably had the meth that was found at his autopsy. I don't think my dad even ever had a drink. He might not have known what being high even felt like."

Georgia took a drink from the water glass on the little table that sat in the middle of the deck chairs and continued.

"I shouldn't tell you this, and you should burn this letter after you read it. But there were two men that came to kill me. A few months apart. Mike said the demon spirits possessed them. They are in two of the mannequins. Their spirits are. Drifters he said. I don't know. I don't remember killing them. I found them already dead. I must have cut their throats. But I think the good spirits let me forget. That's what Mike says. He's been such a good friend. My only friend. But I can't tell him everything. I think he knows about the money. But I can't be sure. The bins Georgia. Mike won't go looking in them. I told him about all the spiders. He can handle demons but not spiders. Isn't that funny? When I found the gold bars, I built the shed to cover the hole. They were so heavy I sold them for cash. I don't need much. I don't want much. I can't bring back your mom and Grace, but I can give you that. The bad guys are in the attic now, but I hope to have them gone before you ever see them. But things have been so…fast. When I try, I keep getting distracted. I've hid them in the room where I keep the demons I've trapped. They are starting smell something awful. It makes it hard to eat, but I'm never that hungry anyway. I sealed up the room and attic, so it doesn't stink in the house. But Mike says I have to leave them there. I don't like to defy him, because he gets mad and I'm afraid he'll stop bringing the herbs. He's my friend. I think I need them now. I feel so terrible without them. My brain gets slow, and I hurt, and I sleep for days. The herbs bring the spirits. With the herbs I don't need to sleep, the spirits are my energy! Some are good spirits, and some are bad spirits. The bad spirits are in the mannequins. They come from Hell. The good spirits are the ones in my head the most. But they make my heart race. And I can hear the bad spirits whisper at night. They helped fix up the place for you. The good spirits. I am so afraid for your soul Georgia. I know it was Satan that led to make the choices you have made. That is why you must burn the bad spirits. They're demons. Before they take you too. Burn them Georgia, please. P.S. There's something in the bins in the shed. Mike doesn't know. I trust him. I have to because he's my friend, but I didn't tell him because it's got to be yours now. It's the only thing I have. I just want you to be safe in this life and the next."

She stopped because the letter stopped. Eric waited for more.

"Is that it?"

"Looks like it."

"Cash in the bins?"

"Sure. He's delusional, Eric," hoping her tone let him know the subject was fucking closed. She was full up to her ass in secrets, and the last thing she wanted was an old plastic bins filled with ugly sweaters and the mummified hearts of transients. She wasn't buying the gold thing.

Eric nodded, and his phone rang again. He answered it, but didn't get up. After a few 'Really's and 'Okay's, he hung up. "Well, wouldn't you know, Mike and Ann are married."

"What the actual fuck?" Georgia was only shocked for a moment, "Although I guess that tracks. Lots of people from this town end up together. "Wait, who was that?"

"I have a friend that is very good at finding things out," he said. "I sent him a few things to look up. That gold claim is a fake. And like we thought that blog tracks back to Ann. Or her kid anyway. He used a VPN, but my 'friend'" Eric drew out the word, "was able to trace it anyway. It wasn't hidden all that well." He paused, "So, this is my take, Ann and Mike planted the gold claim to help the story seem more legit, set up the blog and drove your dad nuts, The 'herbs' obviously helped. And I don't think your dad killed the people you found. My guess is Mike did and set him up."

"By facilitated, you mean killed him. He didn't know what the fuck he was taking or why it made him feel that way. I swear I didn't think he could kill anybody. So, I guess that is a relief. As far as the gold claim, he probably said some shit about gold bars when he was high and they planted the claim to bolster his fantasy." She still didn't know the guy, but feelings of sorrow had started to bud. Not for the man himself, but what he had been put through. Although, she believed he hadn't really killed anyone, she couldn't know for sure. "Any clue as to why go to all this trouble?"

"Yeah, my friend found some other dirt on Ann. Although, we probably wouldn't have needed him to figure it out. A quick search would show that Ann, specialized in selling "stigmatized" properties. Or tried to anyway."

"Like haunted houses?"

"Yup. She made a killing…" he grinned at the pun. Georgia

rolled her eyes but appreciated the joke even if she didn't want him to know that. "...on a supposed haunted property as one of her first sales. She kept trying to do it again, but never found another with enough of a reputation to make that kind of profit again."

"Did you find out which house it was that she sold?"

"I think he said the Darning House?"

"Danning. It's an old Victorian, up in Kelseyville. It's right in the middle of a historic gold rush town. There's a museum there and a ton of old buildings set up as old time-y shops. There's a blacksmith, and an ice cream shop. My sister worked the ice cream shop one summer, and swore the basement was haunted." Georgia rolled her eyes. The schools do field trips to teach about the gold rush. But mostly it's a tourist trap. The Danning house gives ghost tours. And as far as I know does really well, especially after being featured on just about every ghost hunter show and blog there is."

"So, Ann and Mike were manufacturing a ghost tourist trap? But why let the old guy give you the house? I still don't get that."

"Maybe I was supposed to find the bodies, report them to the police and move out screaming when I *heard* ghosts? My dad said that Mike didn't want him to get rid of the bodies. I mean a couple of extra bodies could go a long way toward attracting the attention of the million or so ghost hunters online."

"But Ann was a cunt to you..."

"Maybe she couldn't help herself, old habits die hard? Maybe she wanted me to freak out and blow up. And maybe she was going to have Mike to step in to buy the fucking thing. He was creepy, but had he made me an offer, I might have taken it. Can't say I would have done that if it had been Ann or if I had known they were married. Maybe she figured that out after she saw me face to face and decided to drop her, *I'm-not-a-cunt after all* act. But I think that's why she didn't call the police when I punched her in the face. She was still hoping I would get scared and dump the house on the first offer, who would be Mike. And I'm going to take a wild guess that Mike is the neighbor that found him."

"Fuck. What a business plan. But they got the whole town to harass your father?"

"Not as hard as you might think. Remember when that chick came in with the weird green hair…."

"Omg! The one with the tiny little third nipple?"

"Yup. Astra. Everyone hated her," Georgia said. "Bullied her right out of the club. I thought she was weird, but customers liked her. I didn't hate her, but I admit I didn't defend her either."

"I get it. It's fucked up, but I get it."

"Easier to either shut the fuck up or be out of the 'Hate Astra' club and risk the wrath of the mob. They all banded around an enemy. But I can honestly say, she didn't deserve that. My father had already been a target of rumors, I think he was just the perfect mark."

"People are dicks," Eric sighed.

"Indeed. But what the fuck do I do now?"

"We."

"Ok, what the fuck do *we* do now?"

"For now, I say we go into the city for some lunch and a movie."

"Really?" Georgia said. "That sounds like a terrible idea."

"Really. We need to be gone from here for a little while." He paused. "At least while the haulers are here. But first we got to look in the bins."

She assumed that the *haulers,* were Ken's people, or fuck, maybe they were Eric's, but if this were a gangster movie, they'd probably be called *fixers*.

"Ok. But if Mike or someone were watching, wouldn't they want to call the police? I mean they would get me as a murderer. Or they really think the there's money or gold on the property and want to find it themselves rather than the cops."

"Maybe, but I don't think that is going to be a problem. We got eyes too." Eric said in a low tone. "When we get back, the place will be clean."

Georgia followed Eric out to the truck, still convinced that the rumors of gold or money were simply to add more depth to the ghost story that would make the place famous among ghost hunters. Eric grabbed the first bin on top, he set it down and flipped off the lid. The thick scent of mildew wafted out. Georgia stared down at the moldering pile of jeans. They appeared to be folded over something. Eric looked at her with a raised eyebrow. Then reached down and lifted up a moldering piece of denim revealing rubber band bound bricks of cash. Georgia stunned said nothing.

They worked quickly through the bins. Tossing the clothing into the bed and stacking what seemed like endless bundles of hundred-dollar bills into the emptied bins. Georgia kept count of the total in her head. Math had never been her thing. At least until she became a stripper, then she found she had a knack for accurately estimating a stack of money in her head. She didn't know if Eric had the same skill and didn't ask. He knew better. A mostly unspoken rule in their community of misfits was to never, ever talk about the money you made or had. And even as he helped her carry her stash up to the attic, he stayed blind to the amount of money they had just discovered.

Georgia closed up the attic entrance just as Eric was checking his watch, "We got to boogie. The haulers will be here soon, and we don't want to be here."

"Okay," she said, trying not to wonder just what kind of favor Ken owed Eric. "I need a shower. But I'll be quick."

Eric nodded, "Me too. I'll be right behind you."

Georgia half jogged back up the walk and into the house. She noticed a white blob under the window. Bird shit, she knew.

Bird shit that happened to look like jizz. A twinge of anxiety crawled into her chest, and if she hadn't been in a hurry, she might have looked closer. But it was just bird shit, she was sure of it.

Georgia rinsed the dead body off of her own, and as she toweled off, Eric came into the bathroom. He stripped and got into the shower behind her. It struck her that this was the first time they had been naked in the same room and not had sex. An ominous development.

Ralph hadn't moved from his dent in the sofa, he lifted his head up as they walked out the door. She looked at him and saw the raccoon in her head. Or rather the raccoon's head.

"Hey, you don't think anyone would come and try to hurt Ralph, do you?"

"I don't. Come on, we need to go. I'll let you pick the movie," he smiled, and it gave her chills. Money could change everything.

She drove her car and sped down the twisting road. She didn't see Pete's truck on the way out. In the city, they stopped for a late lunch before the movie. A dark comedy, that almost held her attention. Eric's darkened form in the theater bothered her. He was on her side, but his shadowed face looked as if it held a dozen secrets. It struck her that she didn't know him all that well. She had worked with him for years. Attended at least four funerals in that time, two ODs, a car accident, and one bodybuilding manager with a steroid habit that caught up with him in the form of an aneurysm in the middle of the night. But she wasn't sure if that meant she really knew the guy. She needed him now, and she couldn't deny that. What she didn't know was if she would need him when all this was over. Although, she was starting to doubt that it would ever be over. The hits just kept coming.

Her dad's truck along with everything in it were gone when they got back. Ralph hadn't moved, which Georgia thought was a good sign. Eric and Georgia went out to the back porch to smoke a joint which they had picked up at a dispensary that was not in the town of Blackberry Ridge. The night air was clear and frigid, but they were bundled up in a couple of thick blankets as they passed the joint back and forth. Two cups of chamomile tea steamed on the little table between them.

"I think I want to pick up his ashes," Georgia's words rode out of her mouth on a cloud of smoke.

"Ok," was all he said.

"I can't say I am mourning him, but I feel like it's something I should do."

"Do you want to spread them somewhere?"

"I think so. I know I definitely don't want to keep them. I didn't know him to miss him. I didn't understand him, but I know I'm not angry at him anymore. He was a very troubled man. And maybe he did the best he could with what he had. I can't change how I grew up, or the things that happened to him or me. Or my sister and mom. But maybe I can do one last thing out of respect if not love or sadness."

"Aren't you curious about his origins? His side of the family and your heritage? The gold bars? Maybe it could give you some closure."

"You know, I'm not. And what is closure anyway? There might not even have been any gold bars. He could have simply hoarded his cash under the table this whole time," she wasn't sure she believed that, but it was one mystery she was going to let stand, if only because she had her fill of solving mysteries for the time being. "I'm sure there's someone on YouTube that would love to give me some bullshit explanation then sell me some program or supplement to find it, but I think it's just a made-up word that means nothing. As far as my heritage? Yeah, I really don't want to know. Why would I? To find out that whatever plagued him, before the meth anyway, is genetic? No, fuck all that. If I'm going to die shitting in my pants and screeching gibberish, I'd rather not know ahead of time."

"Fair enough," Eric said, but as he passed the dwindling joint to her with one hand, he put his other hand on her shoulder.

"I guess my closure is finally letting go of the resentment and anger at my dad. As far as my family goes, that's enough. It has to be. Digging in any further isn't going to help anything. But I am angry at this fucking town, and Mike and Ann. And all the fuckers that joined in the torment for the sake of their 'community'. A bunch of fucking ghouls." She flicked the roach over the railing of the deck and instantly remembered that there was a ton of dry ass leaves down there. "Ooo... that was probably a bad idea." She got up and dumped her tea over where she had dropped the roach. Steam, and not smoke she hoped, rose up into the air.

"Well karma's a bitch," Eric said.

"I don't believe in karma. Sometimes shitty things happen to people who make shitty decisions. And fuck, sometimes shitty things just happen. Good things happen to shitty people as well. If there is some magical system of justice keeping score, it's doing a piss poor job of it."

He shrugged. They went inside. The house, now rid of all it's dead bodies and her father's possessions, felt lighter. Eric felt lighter, the apprehension she had felt in the theater had faded and fucked off to whatever part of her messed up brain it had come from. They made love and fell asleep. Ralph snuck up later and snuggled himself unnoticed between their pillows.

23

"HEY THERE, BUDDY," Eric said as he spit cat hair out of his mouth the next morning. Georgia went to move the furry interloper, but Eric stopped her. "He's fine. Poor thing."

"I guess, I'll go start the coffee."

"Nope, I'll get it," Eric said and kissed her as he walked his naked butt on bare feet to the kitchen. She had hung curtains over the window, but the sunlight powered through them anyway. She laid there and tried to come up with an appropriate place to put her father. She didn't want to do it here, on the property. He might not have seen it that way, but to her, this place was his prison. Or maybe his asylum, but it was this place that trapped him in life. She wanted him to be free. If only symbolically. Anything she did now wouldn't be for him, he was gone. His mind left before his body, but she didn't want his physical remains to be trapped here forever.

Eric came back with the coffee. They sat and sipped it in silence, until Ralph decided he had gotten enough cat hair on the sheets and hopped down.

"I guess I should go feed him," Georgia said.

"Nope, I filled his dish and scooped the box while the coffee was brewing."

She eyed him suspiciously, then leaned over to kiss him. He leaned into it.

"Ok, I'm ready to do this," she got up and went to the shower. When he didn't get up to follow her, she said, "You coming?"

"If it's on the menu," he said with a smile.

After they were showered and dressed, they got in her car and headed again into the town where the crematorium held Ron's ashes. When they got there, she was told that she had gotten there only day before they were to dispose of them. She took the plain cardboard box and thanked the employees, before heading back up the hill.

Georgia parked her car on a scenic turnout on the mountain. Eric pulled out a small knife from his pocket and cut open the box. Inside was a plastic bag full of grey powder. She looked down over the stone fence that had replaced a guardrail that had been broken by one too many drunk drivers. She had no idea how high up it was, but the bottom of the canyon was nearly out of view. A light layer of fog concealed the true distance of the drop. Eric cut the tie holding the bag closed. She took it out and waited for a break in the light breeze. Then she tipped the bag upside down and let Ron's remains float down to wherever they would settle. But wherever that was, it wasn't Blackberry Ridge. They couldn't hurt him anymore.

They rode in silence on the way back in the early afternoon light. Georgia's mind was at peace, she focused only on the road. She didn't think, she didn't want to think. And for once her thoughts cooperated. Until she saw the smoke.

"Fuck there's a fire somewhere," immediately she thought of her careless tossing of the roach and found that the thought of that house burning down didn't bother her. Until Ralph crossed her mind, and she sped up.

"I know what you're thinking, George, and that's not it. If the roach was going to set anything on fire, it would have been last night."

She knew he was right but kept speeding anyway. If only because it was fun. As they got to the junction where one way would take her to the main street of Blackberry Ridge, and the other to her property, she saw the smoke was coming from the town itself. She turned toward the town.

"What are you doing?" Eric said sounding alarmed.

"If the town is burning, I want to see," she said, ignoring his concern.

"Let's not. I'm sure we'll see it in the news or something."

"Yeah, I don't care. I want to see. The black and grey smoke means it's a structure fire. I want to see."

"Please George, let's just go back," Eric said, but it was too late.

They pulled up to the main drag as far as the fire trucks would let them. Which wasn't far. A large crowd had gathered and before he could stop her, she was parked and out of the car. He followed her into the crowd where she had muscled her way to the front. Half of one side of the main drag of Blackberry Ridge was engulfed in flames. But the other side was untouched.

A breathless mostly grey-haired lady in baggy jeans and a flannel shirt standing next to her said without turning her head, "It started at the feed store. They think there might be someone inside."

"See, karma," Eric said, putting his arm gently around her as he tried to lead her out of the crowd and back to her car.

"Yeah, I still don't believe that. The place was full of cardboard and hay, I'm surprised it took this long." she looked one more time at the spreading fire. She wasn't surprised it took this long, though. Fires were a big deal and real threat up here, and the Berry Folk didn't fuck around when it came to fire safety. It was going to take out the whole side of the main drag before they would be able to get it out. But the widened street seemed to be preventing the fire from jumping to the other side. Georgia thought that was a real pity. The flames burned into her retinas, and she allowed Eric to guide her out. When they got back to the car, she looked at him through the fading white blur that put a blank space where his face should be. "Tell me that you didn't have anything to do with that."

"Karma," he said.

"Bullshit," her vision was clearing, and she could see his face again.

"Ok. Let's call it 'facilitated karma.'"

Georgia smiled.

24

RALPH WAS WAITING for them just inside the front door, but rather than try to trip her in order to get her to fill his dish, he ran past them and outside.

"Well, that's weird," Georgia said.

"What?"

"He has refused to go outside other than the back porch," she said.

Ralph was howling and staring out past the shed. He scurried up to the front door and then down the walk and back again.

"Something is out there," Eric said. "And no, I don't think it's a ghost," he rolled his eyes, giving back what she has been throwing his way.

"An animal or something?"

"Yeah, we should go look," he said.

"Can't think of much I'd rather do less...than that," she said but followed him down the walk anyway. When Ralph saw them start to walk in that direction, he darted back inside the house.

The leaves crunched under their feet as they walked toward

the shed. A faint moaning sound was coming from the fence line.

Where she had set the bear trap.

"That doesn't sound like an animal," Eric said.

"Ah, city boy, you just don't...." she was cut off as they neared the edge of the fence.

A shot rang out and she felt something whiz past her face, ruffling her hair. Eric grabbed her by the back of her head and firmly pushed her to the ground. He pulled his knife out of his pocket and crouched down beside her.

Georgia felt the sweat bead up behind her neck and on her chest. As it dripped between her breasts, she saw what was caught in the bear trap. Not an animal. Mike. He sat on the ground awkwardly. His leg was twisted, as his ankle disappeared into the metal mouth of the rusty metal trap. He had the gun trained on them. He looked as if he was going to shoot again but moaned instead.

"Well, I guess you can shoot us and die slowly of sepsis, if the blood loss doesn't get you first. Or you can let us get you out of there," Eric yelled, still crouched down fully expecting another shot. He whispered to her without taking his eyes off the injured man, "That's Mike, isn't it?"

"It is," she whispered back.

"Toss the gun away," Eric called to him.

"Fuck you!" was the response.

"I'm good," Eric said.

"Fuck you!" Mike said again.

"A real wordsmith, this guy," Eric said. "Back up slowly, stay close to the ground. We can't know how many shots he's got, but we can get out of range."

They crawled backwards, keeping close to the ground as one more shot came and went wildly off to the side of them and hitting an old oak. When they got back to the shed, they stood up and Eric pulled his phone out. He opened it and made a call.

"Hello, we need the police and an ambulance," he said, and gave them the address. "Someone had an accident coming onto our property. He's hurt but has a gun and has shot at us." a pause, then, "Okay." He hung up.

"Now you call the police?" Georgia said a little confused.

"Yup. Now we call the police." Eric said to Georgia, then called out to Mike, "We found Ron's note. We know what you did."

Georgia added, kind of lamely, "You fucker!"

They heard the sound of soft footsteps behind them. They turned to see Micheal creeping toward them coming from the house. Georgia's blood froze. The little bastard must have been hiding in the fucking house. The raccoon, the footprint, the bird shit. That she now knew wasn't bird shit. In some weird way, it almost flattered her. The little bastard couldn't have been more than twenty but already corrupted by his fucked-up parents. And he had the biggest knife Georgia had ever seen. He picked up the pace and started running. A loud bang and a hole appeared in his chest as his eyes went wide. Mike hadn't recognized his son and fired on him. Micheal dropped to the ground.

They waited in silence for the ambulance and the police. As they heard the sirens approach, they heard another shot. Georgia didn't wonder what it was. She knew the boy who felt her up all those years ago was gone.

Blackberry Ridge didn't have a police department; it was the county sheriff that showed up shortly after the ambulance. Georgia didn't have to act freaked out. It all came naturally. No mask needed this time. All of the fucked-up emotions and feelings came out in a rush as the sheriff and his deputy walked around, what she hoped would be the last dead bodies on the property. After the scene was processed, the sheriff took her brief statement. She only told them what they needed to know, which wasn't much. She didn't think they needed the letter, it would be ash soon anyway. They took the body away and let them know that they would be in touch if they needed any more information.

Bodies? Rotting corpses? No officer, nothing like that here as far as I know. Just a bunch of ugly ass sweaters in the shed.

"Is it still going to be okay?" Georgia asked as they sat on the sofa. Her head rested on his shoulder, while Ralph sat on her lap.

"It's going to be better than okay. Karma remember?"

"Facilitated karma you mean."

"Yeah, that." Eric kissed the top of her head. "I said I was going to make it all okay, and it will be. Do you still believe me?"

"I don't see that I have much of a choice."

"I'll take it." He kissed her again. But this time on the mouth.

Georgia's phone woke her the next morning, a call from the sheriff. She put it on speaker.

"Ms. Duran?"

"Yes," she said.

"We have some more information about the incident on your property. The intruder was the owner of the feed store where the fire started in town yesterday. They found a body that appears to have been shot with the same caliber of gun that the man found on your property was in possession of. We don't have all the pieces yet, but we'll let you know when we have more information. We have the wife in custody, as she appears to have been involved. We believe they were trying to acquire the property."

She thanked him and disconnected.

"See? It's all going to be okay." Eric said, taking her into his arms. Ralph hadn't left them alone since alerting them the day before, he slept on the end of the bed.

Georgia desperately believed that it was going to be okay. But there was the nagging fact of how it all came to be okay. She knew better than to ask. If she had learned anything at all from these past few weeks, it was that knowing too much was like the worst thing ever. Ignorance and bliss and all that was going to be her new life's mantra. She had resolved herself to the fact that she was going to have a boyfriend, whether she liked it or not. And the more she thought about it, the less scary the thought itself became.

Georgia looked over at Eric, lying and staring up at the ceiling. A view she now herself tried to avoid. Ralph had crawled up on top of him and laid on his chest with his snout just below Eric's chin. She could hear him purring. She took a deep breath and asked him just what he was involved in with Ken. Maybe bliss wasn't going to be her thing.

"Drugs. Heroin mostly. But a little meth here and there, ketamine for sure. Molly obviously. Ken has a couple of plants in each high school in the northern half of the state. They create a steady stream of new customers. Fentanyl is all the rage you know. Very loyal customers. And young. Occasionally things go bad, and I need to clean some stuff up for him. Get rid of problems if you catch my drift. The club hides the money. Cops are paid off. Pretty standard."

Georgia's eyes flew open, and she let out the breath she had been holding, "What?"

"Coffee, George. Are you ready for coffee?" Eric said. "If you're not, I don't want to disturb Ralph." It took her a moment to realize she had made up a whole conversation in her head.

"Fuck," she said, coming back out of her head. "Yeah, but I'll get it."

She leaned over and kissed him. She walked out to the kitchen and started the coffee. Georgia knew, or at least she knew the stereotype, of strip club owners and drugs or whatever. Like every strip club in every movie was owned by one kind of gangster or another. Was she making the same assumptions as everyone else did? Perpetuating stereotypes. She didn't know for sure. And she decided she didn't want to. Not ever. Eric might be ass deep in whatever Ken was doing, but so far, she had only stuck in a pinky toe, and that was all she could spare. Bliss Georgia desperately wanted, as she wanted to believe it was going to all be okay, she wanted sweet ignorant bliss. She had enough money to do whatever she wanted. She just didn't know what that was yet. And the money was dirty. She really didn't know and certainly couldn't explain where it had come from. She hadn't sat on enough tax lawyers lap yet to know the implications of declaring her dead father's hoarded cash.

Georgia carried two steaming mugs of coffee into the bedroom, where Ralph had already moved to the foot of the bed. Eric sat up with his back against the pillows and took his mug from her.

"Do you want to come stay with me George?" Eric asked quietly. "My place isn't very big, but I think we can find a bigger place if you want. Or you can just stay there until you find something else."

She sipped her coffee, then kept sipping as her thoughts ran in circles. Lately her thoughts had become harder to control. As all this kept unfolding, a horrid tendril of realization kept winding its way through her mind. She was following the footsteps of her father. Her mind was slipping, she could blame it on hormones, but each vivid vision, nightmare, or paranoid fantasy was simply her brain losing its grip. She was slipping. Sure, she smoked a lot of herb, but deep down that wasn't it. She was her father's daughter, and she didn't have to google it to know that mental illness was hereditary. It didn't help that she hadn't had health insurance or been to a real doctor in several years. She didn't want to burden Eric with all that, but she didn't want to be in this house anymore either. She also, wasn't all that excited to be alone. A feeling as alien as the sudden flashes of heat that plagued her now.

"I think that might work if you don't mind Ralph coming

along, the little fucker has grown on me. And I think it might take a while to either sell this place, and for me to find a job," she said finally.

"It will all sort itself out in time. I promise," he said. "And the fur ball has grown on me too, I guess. Always considered myself more of a dog person though."

"Well, I'm thinking it would be temporary," she wasn't sure she was thinking that, but the thought of a firm commitment still riled her guts.

"That will sort itself out in time too," he leaned over and kissed her. "Let's finish the coffee and get the fuck out of here."

"I really like that plan."

Georgia took his mug from him and set it on her nightstand. They rolled around in the sheets until Ralph got the hint and left for his sanctuary on the sofa. After they showered and dressed, he helped her pack up as much as she could carry in both of their vehicles and left the house at Blackberry Ridge.

25

SHE HAD NEVER BEEN to Eric's house. But it was a house. Not an apartment. And it was much bigger than her own house and definitely bigger than her apartment. As she looked around the spartan décor and furniture, she understood why he recognized the Ikea furniture in the attic immediately. It appeared he furnished his entire house that way. Except for the antique sewing table he explained had come from his grandmother and still held her yarn. But it was clean. At least until Ralph was let out of the carrier and hopped on the sofa to deposit some of his hair. She had expected him to rebel or fight, or seem at least perturbed, but as soon as his butt found the middle cushion of the sofa, he looked like he owned the place.

"So, I guess I shouldn't have been so worried if he would settle in okay," Eric said as he sat next to the cat on his newly commandeered sofa.

"Dude. I think it was Mike. Like I think he was afraid of him," Georgia said.

Ralph didn't chime in, but he did open one eye at the mention of Mike.

"I don't know, but he sure looks comfortable now," Eric said and scratched the scruff of Ralph's neck. "I'm thinking we should keep him inside though, we're set pretty far back from the street, but cars could be a problem."

She just nodded.

Georgia didn't bother with the guest room, except to store her things. But most of her things were still at the house in Blackberry Ridge. It took her just slightly longer to settle in than Ralph but when she was done, she joined Eric and Ralph on the sofa. Eric had a UFO documentary on his TV. Ralph kept his eyes closed but began to purr when she sat down on the other side of him.

"Do you think the cops are going to search the house?" She asked, instantly wishing she hadn't.

"I don't," he said. "But I need to tell you a few things."

She felt a flash of heat rise up from her chest, as if the flames of Hell were coming to get her. She removed her thin sweatshirt, freezing the sweat on her breast, and promptly put it back on again.

"Ken is…"

"Yeah, I don't want to know." She interrupted. "Being informed is highly overrated," she stopped looking at him and started to pet the sleeping Ralph.

"For real, you do need to know a few things, if only for the sake of transparency. Like I said, if you want to run out of here screaming…actually don't do that, the neighbors might get pissed and I don't think they like me already… you can. But I got to tell you just a few things. If you hate me or want to bail, I'll put you up in a place until you find something else."

"Doesn't sound like I can stop you, I guess," She held her breath as he began to speak.

"So, the cops aren't going to call you again. Any investigation that was open is closed. As far as they are concerned, the bodies your dad mentioned were like you said, just the ravings of a crazy old man. That part is done. In fact, if you don't ever want to go back there, you don't have to. We can have everything picked up."

"Ken?" She said without looking up.

"I thought you didn't want to know?"

"I don't."

"Then I won't tell you." He said and she knew then that small town cops were probably pretty easy to bribe.

"Okay, that it?" she said, hoping it was, but knowing it wasn't.

Georgia looked up from Ralph, as Eric continued to talk faster than she had ever heard him. Obviously trying to get it all out, before she freaked the fuck out.

"I'm listening," she was slightly terrified thinking he would reveal the details of Ken's business. She didn't want to know. Not ever.

"He'd like to buy the property. He's already making arrangements to buy the burned-out part of the town and probably the rest of it too. He said he would give you final say on what happens to the house. If you care." She didn't.

She kept petting Ralph, who had flipped over on to his back and exposed his most tender bits. Georgia still didn't believe in signs, but she knew that cats didn't show their bellies unless they felt safe. And it was hard to not take it as some sort of a sign. She had already flipped over and allowed Eric to rub her belly. She had let him take over and given up a measure of her control. And control, was all she had when she left Blackberry Ridge the first time. She had allowed Eric to break in, to breach her walls, and it terrified her. At least at first, and even as she tried to talk herself out of it, he made her feel safe. She could no longer pretend that he didn't. She'd spent over half of her life as a hard ass. Pushing away everyone who attempted to get close to her, swimming in the belief that she didn't need anyone. That it was Georgia against the world and fuck everyone else. Now she was drowning in the realization, that all she ever wanted was to feel safe. To feel cared for. To feel accepted for who she was. To feel loved. *Fuck. Puke.*

"Well, I'd probably be a total asshole to turn that down. But I need to know, Eric. I need to know just one thing. I know I've got some antisocial tendencies, but I really don't like the idea of hurting people. So, I just need to know one thing, not details, just ballpark it for me." She paused, stealing herself for the answer that might make her turn down Ken's offer. But she didn't want to take it without knowing. Fuck her bliss. "Is what he does, or what he's involved with hurt anyone?" She was thinking drugs, trafficking, murder.

"If you're thinking hard drugs or sex trafficking, the answer is no. Look, I'm not completely apprised of the goings on myself. Like you, I like to keep an air of mystery. But to my knowledge, he or his organization hasn't hurt anyone."

"Just facilitated karma," she said.

"Probably that, yes, but like you said people make their own karma. Right?"

"That's not exactly what I said, but yeah. I suppose. "So, he's not taking out soccer moms at the grocery store or hooking little kids on drugs and selling them to old men?"

"Definitely not that. Anyway, as far as me and Ken go, we're square. Our business is finished."

Ralph had enough of the belly pets and drew back and caught the meaty part of her hand in his jaws. Chomping down just hard enough for her to take the hint but not hard enough to draw blood.

"Ow, fucker," she said. It didn't hurt. She looked at the tiny poke marks and thought for a few minutes. What to Eric must have seemed like an eternity. But he simply sat in silence next to her. Here was her way out. Her conscience was clear, for the most part. "Well, I wouldn't want to be a total asshole. But I want to talk to him myself."

Ralph sensing what was about to happen jumped off the sofa

in a huff, and presumably went to spread more cat hair throughout Eric's virgin house. Eric leaned over and hugged her. Then kissed her.

"Oh shit! I forgot to tell you. Although that is mostly your fault. Considering all your drama. Jake made up those flyers. Ken had nothing to do with it. There are no restrictions on shifts. He's going to get fired.

"No!" she blurted, and Eric looked confused. She lowered her tone, "I want to do it."

Georgia knew exactly what she wanted.

EPILOGUE

Georgia sat behind her dark mahogany desk. The finish was almost exactly like the mahogany counter at the county library where she and Eric began to unravel the mystery of her father's land. It was vintage. An antique rolltop from the late twenties. She didn't know she was in to antiques until she started to refurbish and completely remake Cherry's Gentleman's club.

The price she got for her father's property would have been, if she had planned carefully, enough to retire. It was 'fuck you' money. She felt like what she got was more than fair. But retirement didn't appeal to her. She had negotiated to take over the club. She had no idea what her vision was for herself or her future, but when the opportunity came to burn it all down and start over fresh, a vision for the club became clear. She had faith her own transformation would follow.

The transfer of ownership of both the house and the club was pretty easy. Ken's lawyers set it up so that there would be no loose ends, and that was it. She had sat down with Ken, the strip club owner, she had never met and negotiated the whole thing on her own. A feeling of power she hadn't known fully clothed. The club would make an excellent laundromat as Ken himself was aware. She hadn't told him about the cash, but the looks they traded told her he knew. Ken could keep a secret. Or a hundred. They swapped properties and that was all that had to be said and arranged.

Her father and the Berry Folk were behind her for good now. The memories of the place had faded like the scent of the new paint in the office where she currently sat with Ralph on her lap. Ralph hadn't quite settled into his new home as Georgia and Eric had hoped. In fact, it had only taken him three weeks to shred nearly the entire sofa. So, she had started to take him to work with her. The renovations and construction hadn't bothered him, but he didn't like to be left alone. Now as she petted him in her lap on opening night, the little fucker wore a bow tie to match her fitted twenties-style girl gangster pinstriped suit.

Watching the town burn had been cathartic, but firing Jake made her feel like she owned the whole fucking world. The look on his face was worth more money than her father could have fit in the shed. She waited with his last check in his hand for him to come into her office. She had let him twist and wind himself in knots as he planted his lips on her ass after finding out she was now his boss. When she finally ended his suffering, she couldn't tell if it was relief, tears, or sheer rage in his eyes. In the end she just didn't give a shit.

But the reality was, she did Jake a favor. His days of manipulating naivete were over, and even if she had kept him on, his pool of victims would be dried up. Her changes didn't consist of just a new stage and new velour for the couches. Cherry's would become a 1920s style bar and burlesque club. She had done her research, and the vintage speakeasy, with its lurid façade of danger and risqué performances were the new thing. And she had money to play with, if it failed. But she didn't think it would. She retained most of her performers, at least the ones who wanted to work with a choreographer on their shows and become employees. Not all of them wanted that, and those who didn't were given bonuses and a sincere thank you from the Eric, the new general manager. Hell's Belles Burlesque lounge offered all of their staff full benefits. The ones she suspected might be giving extras, she left alone. She really couldn't be sure that she her suspicions weren't based on her own insecurities anyway. She'd been wrong before, but she set up the floor in a way that any undue fuckery in the VIP wouldn't go unnoticed or unaddressed.

Georgia fought going to the doctor, still trying to embrace her ignorant bliss, but finally gave in to Eric's urging. Sitting on the exam table, waiting for the doctor was a nightmare that gave the vision of the broken ceiling and her father's maggot filled phantom a run for its fucking money. She was simply terrified. So much in fact, that she was stepping down from the paper covered table and about to not run but walk briskly out of the office and never look back. But then the doctor came in.

Her doctor was kind, and informed. Something she thought all doctors were. Or at least they were supposed to be. But when it came to women of a certain age, Georgia learned that the field of women's sexual health was a new one. Not new like a hundred years or so, but new like only a few decades. Particularly when it came to premenopausal women and what they experienced. Georgia had spent some time before choosing this doctor, and in that time had become slightly enraged at how little concern was given. She had feared that her memory and anxiety and even nightmares, were a symptom of whatever her father had passed on to her. But her physician, Dr. Saint as it were, had run every damn test there was, and finally concluded that everything she was experiencing was totally normal. And correctible. Of course, nothing in science or medicine is a hundred percent, Dr. Saint was confident that she would not suffer the cognitive decline as her father had. Not being unknowingly fed herbs laced with methamphetamine was definitely going to be a big help. What she got instead was a tailored cocktail of estrogen, progesterone, and touch of testosterone. Her hot flashes were gone, as was the anxiety, and weird paranoid visions that had haunted her. Dr. Saint couldn't guarantee that she wouldn't end up screaming at garden gnomes and pissing herself, but she felt it was highly unlikely. Dr. Saint was confident that Georgia had dodged her father's genetic bullet.

Georgia was anxious now. Only twenty minutes until showtime. The floor was packed. Specialty drinks were flowing and the buzz that her new media specialist, the stripper formally known as Sativa, had created was impressive. They were turning people away at the door, if only to appease the fire marshal. Georgia would be out soon to announce the first act. But that wasn't making her anxious. The small black box in her hand did.

She opened it and closed it and tried to steady her hand as she did. Hearing the lid snap closed, then the tiny little creak as she opened it again, then snap closed. If she didn't stop, she was going to break the hinge.

A soft knock came at the door, "Come in," she said.

"Hey babe, how ya doing? You almost ready?" Eric said, looking ridiculously handsome in his pinstriped vest and newsboy hat.

"I am. Fuck me, do you ever look good. Quite the dapper hunk of meat," she said.

"Why thank you. It is jumping down there. The girls are all ready to go, they are so excited, and not one of them smells like vodka. Not even Coco."

She laughed, "It's kind of amazing what the peace of mind of having a having a steady paycheck does for one's drinking habits."

"Not to mention health insurance, I haven't seen one bottle of essential oil or healing crystal since you reopened the dressing room. You did a really good thing, George." He closed his eyes for a moment, "I'm so fucking proud of you."

Tears pricked her eyes, she said almost under her breath, "Thank you." Georgia couldn't remember anyone, since her mother tell her they were proud of her.

"Holy shit, what a night!" He said and began to walk around the desk, but she set Ralph on the floor and met him before he could get there. He started to say something, but she put a soft finger to his lips to quiet him. She had so much she wanted to say to him, but as she looked into his eyes, all her words left her. So, she kissed him instead, hoping her lips would convey the message her brain refused to.

With only ten minutes before she would introduce Hell's Belles first ever stage show, Georgia kneeled down on one knee. Looking up at Eric, she opened the little black box that held the ring.

ADDITIONAL BOOKS

BY ERIN LOUIS

<u>FICTION</u>

STRIPPER NOIR

with Armand Rosamilia

SOUTH OF HEAVEN

HELL AWAITS

COLLEEN

DIRTY THOUGHTS AND AWKWARD BONERS

Sexy Short Stories by a Former Stripper

<u>NONFICTION</u>

EXPOSE YOURSELF

How to Take Risks, Question Everything, and Find Yourself

ABOUT THE AUTHOR

Erin Louis is a former exotic dancer, with a love of books, writing and humor. She spent twenty years as a stripper on and off and started writing as a way to shed light on a misunderstood industry and profession. Frustrated with the stereotypes often presented on talk shows, movies, and articles, her goal is to help paint a broader and more accurate picture of the profession and to destigmatize and humanize those who choose to work in the adult entertainment industry. Her passion for writing began with nonfiction, but she has always loved horror fiction. Stephen King, Lois Duncan, and Clive Barker got her through some tough years growing up. She found an escape through those books along with countless others. Her own fiction reflects those influences as well as her love for all things dark and maybe just a bit scary.